SURFER, SAILOR, SMUGGLER

Aloha
Lindsey!

Cheers to
Sailing &
welcome to
kauai!

♡

Melissa

SURFER, SAILOR, SMUGGLER

TALES OF LIVING

MELISSA BUROVAC

ISBN: 978-0-9903820-6-5 (paperback)

978-0-9903820-7-2 (ebook)

LCCN: 2018912098

Wanderers Press

Koloa, HI

"Nothing ruins a good story like an eyewitness."

ALSO BY MELISSA BUROVAC_

Look for these titles by Melissa Burovac:

Wandering

Sylvie Writes a Romance (Book One of the Sylvie's Romance Series)

Sylvie Falls in Love (Book Two of the Sylvie's Romance Series)

This story is a work of fiction, based loosely on hazy memories, fish tales, and rumors. Any truth is probably coincidence.

FOREWORD_

Stepping aboard the *Noel Mae*, a Polaris 43 double ender named after the skipper's mother, the first thing you might notice is the smile of her owner and captain, Rod — bright and welcoming for friends and strangers alike. If you walk down the pier at Kauai's main harbor, regardless of the time of day, you're likely to see a small crowd on the deck of *Noel Mae*; no formal occasion is necessary. At some point everyone is drawn to the boat to see if Rod is home, regardless of whatever reason brought them to the harbor in the first place. Stopping by to say hello invariably leads to cocktails with music playing in the background and, depending upon the weather, it often leads to a day spent sailing around the east side of Kauai enjoying the sunshine and trade winds, or simply sitting onboard talking story until well after the colors of the sunset have faded to a starry black. Rod may not have much in terms of worldly possessions, but he has enough aloha to supply the world.

I met Rod in grade school in Encinitas, California, just north of San Diego. We lived in Cardiff-by-the-Sea, a classic picture-perfect surf town in the 1950s and '60s. It was a tight-knit community of families and local businesses back then; locals enjoyed the ocean during their time off work, and the now-famous surf spots spawned a few professionals, as well as a multitude of excellent surfers who simply had a passion for riding waves. Eventually, our small town became a tourist destination not only for the waves, but for the welcoming atmosphere and beautiful scenery of the Pacific Ocean with a beach walk and tide pools to explore. To Rod, Cardiff was the ultimate playground: with the ocean in front and the cliffs behind, it was a great place for an adventurous boy to grow up.

I gravitated toward Rod because his life, even at that young age, was so much different than mine. I was the only child of two doctors; my parents loved me and provided everything I needed, but their grueling work schedules ensured that I was left with a babysitter — a teenage girl who spent endless hours talking on the phone, constantly twirling the long black cord back and forth on her index finger, while I did homework or watched TV — and later, as a latch-key kid. Rod's family was the exact opposite. He had four siblings — a play-group unto themselves — a stay-at-home mom, and a motorcycle-policeman father who taught the kids how to dive for fish and abalone on his days off. They were a hands-on family, adventuring together, often fighting as kids do, but always affectionate and loving. While my parents were good people and did their best for me, I secretly wished I had been born into Rod's family. I'm ashamed to admit that in times of adolescent anger, usually after a hurried call from the hospital instructing me on what leftovers to heat up for dinner because yet another emergency arose, I ungratefully flung that desire at whichever parent happened to be on the phone. I cringe to think about it now, more so because I have made many calls like that to my own son.

Rod and I couldn't have been more opposite in our youth, and it holds true to this day. As a child of affluent parents, I never wanted for anything materialistic; I only had to say *I wish I had a …* and whatever had caught my eye was given as a well-meaning substitute for time and attention. I had every Matchbox car, Tonka truck, G.I. Joe ever made; my toy chest may as well have said "For one player only" on the side.

With only one working parent, and a civil servant at that, Rod's family never had much money. I'd show up to school on Monday to proudly show off my new Etch-A-Sketch and Rod would be interested for a polite amount of time, taking a few moments to draw his interpretation of boobs as best he could with the dials, then relate how he and his sister spent the weekend in the ocean hanging onto their father's surf-board, taking turns diving to the reef. He described the bright colors of the fish and how they slowly parted as he swam

2

through their schools, spotting an octopus hiding in a hole, catching his first lobster bare-handed and the praise of his family as they boiled it for a celebratory dinner that evening.

Lunch hour at school was the worst time of day to be a kid with poor parents. Looking at the contents of thoughtfully prepared lunch boxes was enough to incite envy, but for less fortunate kids, putting up with the jeers of bullies who never let them forget they had parents who could only afford a single sandwich with no snacks was worse. While Rod never had much in the way of treats in his brown paper sack, and this alone should have made him a target, his lunches instead added to his grade school popularity. Because of his father's diving, he always had lobster tails, abalone sandwiches, or fresh fish — delicacies usually reserved for special occasions for the rest of us. Barely a day went by without someone approaching Rod with a peanut butter and jelly or a bologna sandwich, maybe even with the crusts cut off, asking if he'd like to trade for his lobster swimming in butter and herbs. Sometimes he traded; even back then, he instinctively understood that sharing what you had, regardless of whether you got something as good in return, was the right thing to do. He didn't do it to make friends; he was the rare boy that everyone wanted in their circle, regardless of social standing. As for me, I traded my lunches so people would like me, or so I wouldn't get stuffed in a locker when a teacher wasn't in the hallway.

I never understood why Rod wanted to be my friend — he had so many. I wasn't anything special, not a jock or a stoner or a musician, just a regular kid. I was pretty smart, but Rod didn't care enough about school to bother cheating from me on tests or asking to copy my homework, although I would have gladly let him. Every day we sat together in classes and at lunch, and I was happy in our friendship.

One day in the cafeteria I was showing off my new watch — my very first wristwatch. My parents bought it for me as a special gift; I was finally deemed old enough to be given a key to the house and make my own way, instead of walking home to meet the babysitter. To me, the watch was my first rite of passage on the way to adulthood, nearing 13 years old. To my parents, it served as a reminder to get home, spend time on homework, then heat up my dinner if they didn't arrive home before then. I can't remember now if it was Flintstones, or maybe Jetsons, but no one else I knew had one, which I thought made it even more special.

I specifically remember that day, since Rod had a more exotic lunch than usual: rabbit. Who brings rabbit to school for lunch? He had killed it himself in the foothills behind his house with his own .22 rifle, and his mom cooked it and wrapped it in wax paper, the juices leaking out through the brown paper bag and leaving a scented, greasy smear on the shelf above the coat hooks. My journey toward being a man was nothing like his; instead of homework after school, he went hunting with his older brother. I decided then and there that I would disobey my parents and, if Rod would let me, follow him home from school to learn about a world I couldn't read about in my textbooks.

That plan lasted exactly one day. Rod was overjoyed when I asked to walk home from school with him; he introduced me to his mother — a tall, beautiful woman who smelled like fresh-baked cookies — then we hiked through the hills while he excitedly pointed out where he was hiding when he shot his rabbit, and various boulders he liked to climb to just sit and watch the world go by. So many kinds of birds flying between trees! I was so caught up in the mystery of this new place, so close to my own home yet never glimpsed, that I forgot about my new wristwatch — all I could think of such a short time ago. When Rod pointed out an owl flying low over the scrubby brown grass, he mentioned that it was getting late and we should be heading home for dinner.

The time! It was hours past when I should have been home, should have had my homework done. Rod led me along the path back to his house and invited me to stay for dinner, but instead I ran the blocks to get to my house before my parents suspected I had abused my new freedom. I pulled my house key out from under my t-shirt where it hung around my neck on a thin leather cord, but the door opened before I reached the lock. My mother, still in her blue hospital scrubs that gave off the faintest odor of bodily fluids and bleach and maybe disapproval, towered in the doorway and I knew I was in big trouble.

"Where have you been?" she asked, calmly but in an ice-cold voice. "I called the house every 10 minutes to make sure you got home." Her face was red, and her expression changed from worry to relief to anger as she assessed me top to bottom with her doctor's eye to make sure I was unhurt.

"I went for a walk with my friend," I barely managed to squeak out. I think we were both surprised that I had disobeyed the direct orders from my parents.

"And when did we discuss that? Which friend? Where did you go? You were told to come straight home, have a snack, and start your homework. Is your homework done?"

I wasn't very practiced in the art of deception yet, just a little white lie now and again about trivial things like candy bars and peeping at dirty pictures boys sometimes smuggled into school — although that was really a lie of omission, but who would tell that to their parents? It was quite obvious I hadn't come home at all since I had my book bag slung over my shoulder, so I confessed. It wasn't like I did anything

5

bad, I just went for a walk. To my mom, it didn't matter though.

"You disobeyed our rules; maybe you aren't old enough to be on your own yet — I'll see if Julie can babysit again until you show me you're a responsible young man. And who is this boy you went home with? Do I know his mother?"

I begged and pleaded and cried to retain the freedom I had been granted, and which I had so quickly thrown away. The final decision was made when I remembered to mention that Rod's dad was a policeman, which served to teach me my first lesson in the creative use of facts — I'd never even caught a glimpse of him. My mother relented on the threat of the babysitter, knowing that I really was a good kid, and besides, I was with a policeman's son. The new conditions of keeping my house key were that I would be home directly after school to answer the phone, and any random phone calls which could occur at any time after that, all my homework would be finished, and I was not to watch TV for an entire week — "If the television feels warm when I get home I'll know." I also wasn't allowed back to Rod's house until my mother could meet his mother.

I was the model child over the next few weeks so I could recapture my semi-adult status at home, and instead lived vicariously through Rod and his lunchtime stories of hunting, fishing, and diving. He had gotten his first surfboard and began spending nearly all his spare time in the ocean on weekends catching waves instead of fish. He invited me along, offering to teach me on a board borrowed from his sister. I wasn't a very athletic kid and would have liked to try, but my parents were certain I would break my arm or drown. They took me to the San Diego Natural History Museum that weekend instead.

Rod loved to talk about the owls that lived in the sandstone cliffs near his house flying through the fields halfway between the ocean and the mountains. He knew all about the other birds in the area, but the owls were his favorites, soaring low over the brush in search of prey in the evenings. During a particularly long lull in the surf, his curiosity led him in search of where the owls made their nests; he spent evenings staring at the face of a cliff until he chanced to see an owl emerge from a small cave, just big enough for an owl to roost. He couldn't see inside unless he climbed up the cliff or rappelled down, so the next day after school he hiked to the top, tied a rope around a tree, and peeked inside. I'd never seen him so excited as when he told me what he had found; his eyes sparkled and he could barely stay in his chair.

"Teeny, tiny, fuzzy baby owlets!" he gushed, not caring who heard him nearing the edge of baby-talk. "Five of the cutest little balls of fluff with beaks, making tiny peeping sounds for their momma!"

He closed his eyes and tilted his head toward the ceiling, peeping in imitation of the baby owls.

If I had acted like this within earshot of any of the bigger boys, I would have instantly been called a sissy and beaten up.

Each day at school I received a progress report on the growth of the chicks from Rod's evening hike, although nothing measurable could be reported in so short a time — usually just more peeping sounds. Then Rod was absent for two days.

After school on that second day, I called my mother at work and told her Rod had been sick, and asked permission to bring his homework to his house — an actual real lie, this time; Rod rarely ever did his homework. I figured he wouldn't care if I came over, and if he really was sick maybe I could cheer him up. Getting the okay, and worried my mom

7

might call right back to change her mind, I practically ran to his house. Sick people and homework were two important things to her, but I wasn't taking any chances.

Rod's mother let me in and I instantly felt excitement in the air. The Beach Boys' *Surfin' Safari* was playing on the record player in the corner of the living room, and forming a circle in front of it were Rod and his four siblings, all staring at the carpeted floor like they were huddled around a board game. No one appeared sick, and nobody even looked up to see who was at the door, so I stood there indecisively until Rod's mother gently pushed me toward the group. When I could see into the circle, my jaw dropped and I froze again.

A light blue bath towel was formed into a fluffy cotton nest, and in the middle sat a baby owl no bigger than could fit in the palm of my hand, fast asleep. Rod's oldest sister nudged him in the side and he finally noticed I was in his house; he instantly made room for me in the circle and motioned me to sit down. He had the same wide, happy grin on his face that he always did — he was definitely not sick.

I took my place in the circle between Rod and his youngest sister, only a year younger than us. When I crossed my legs, my knee touched her knee, and I could smell the faintest trace of her coconut tanning lotion — it was years before anyone would be concerned with skin cancer and thought to use sunblock. She had sun-bleached blonde hair and perpetually wore a bathing suit and cut-off denim shorts, as if she was always just about to go to the beach. She was my first crush, although I don't think I ever worked up the courage to speak three words to her in my entire life.

"You'll never believe what happened!" he started, words tumbling out of his mouth almost faster than I could comprehend them, and dragging me back from thoughts of his sister's knee. "I was hiking out back and watching the owls when these kids with a shotgun shot at them and killed one! It went down and they were cheering, and I wanted to go beat them up, but I thought I should get my brother first. So I ran back here to get him and remembered the poor little babies — what if that was their momma they killed? So I hiked up to the top and watched for hours, and momma owl never came back. I could hear the poor little babies crying from the peak. I bet they were hungry."

He paused for just a moment to catch his breath. "Mom wouldn't let me go back and get them at night, so first thing the next morning I packed some stuff and climbed up. I hammered some tent spikes into the cliff so I could tie my rope off all the way down and hang a basket on the ledge. Then I crawled in the cave and there they were, all five, just peeping away with their mouths open." He tilted his head back and made more peeping sounds, but mournful, minor-key peeps this time.

His grinning face changed to a look of deep sadness, almost as if he were about to cry. "The poor little owl babies with no one to look after them now. I didn't want them to die. I wrapped them in this towel and put them in the basket and climbed back up." Rod mimed climbing up the cliff face, placing the wooden handle of the basket on each successive spike until he reached the top.

"Mom said we couldn't keep them, and that we should take them to the Humane Society," he said, then quickly glanced at his mother sitting on the couch nearby with a look of reproach. "But I told her I had saved them, and I could be a momma owl and teach them to hunt, and they wouldn't be far from their home when they were ready to go back. She finally said yes, but I could only keep one, and she took the other four away. I hope they know how to take care of them there."

He turned his attention back to the owl nestled in the towel; I still hadn't said anything.

"Wow" was all I could think of.

Ceramic bowls of different colors were placed near the outside of the towel, each containing something I couldn't quite identify, and books were strewn about the room, open at seemingly random pages. I picked up the closest one to me, *All About Birds*.

"We went to the library and checked out every bird book so we know how to take care of Alfie."

"Alfie? How can you tell it's a boy?"

"Well, I can't, but I like the name. And he's brown, and that seems like a boy color."

"But the girls would be brown too, wouldn't they?"

"It's still Alfie," Rod replied after a moment of thought. "He's a barn owl, and the books say they eat mice and fish and other birds, but insects, too. So mom went to Vann's and brought home some bits of meat and had the butcher grind up bones, and we all went out back and caught all the bugs we could find," he indicated at a container covered with a dish towel; he pulled off the towel, revealing a glass jar with holes poked in the lid containing numerous insects crawling over each other at the bottom. "We've been trying everything to see what he likes best."

The little bird awoke, his frightened eyes not quite seeing but instinctively knowing he wasn't in his nest in the cliffs. He began to peep, not quite as sadly as Rod had imitated, eliciting whimpering noises from Clancy, the black labrador retriever looking on from across the room. Clancy had tried to get into the circle earlier and had been banished to his dog bed.

"He'll get used to us soon, I think. We're playing him music and talking to him when he's awake."

One of Rod's sisters squeezed a single drop of water at a time into Alfie's begging mouth with an eyedropper, then followed up with a small piece of ground meat. The peeping continued, and we took turns feeding the fragile bird from the various bowls.

"Mom says we can't feed him bugs inside the house in case they get away." Again, Rod shot a glare at his mother, who smiled in return. She was reading one of the bird books, obviously as excited about this family project as her kids were.

I sat enthralled until the house began to grow dim and I realized it was nearing sunset. I had to be home before dark, and wasn't about to get caught disobeying again and missing out on the owl's progress by being grounded.

"Will you be at school tomorrow?" I asked Rod. "I think we have a geography quiz."

Rod began to shake his head 'no,' but his mother answered for him. "Yes, he will." When Rod opened his mouth to protest, she calmly continued, "I've let you spend two days with Alfie, but now it's time to go back. I'm perfectly capable of watching a baby bird. You can't miss a quiz."

I walked home, amazed — not only about the owl, but at the loving atmosphere of Rod's house. I told my parents about the rescued owl, asking for permission to visit every day after school as a learning experience; they allowed me one day per week and I happily accepted. I kept my jealous thoughts about his family to myself.

I didn't see Alfie as frequently as I would have liked, so his fast growth was measurable at my weekly visits. The weeks turned into months, Alfie put on weight and learned to fly, and school was days away from closing for summer break. Most kids await summer with poorly concealed excitement, but not me. I was to be shipped off to science camp in 10 days to spend an entire month without my best friend and his owl — and his sun-kissed sister — although I never had a chance to repeat our knee touching experience no matter how slyly I tried.

On my final visit to Rod's house before I left, a beautiful sunny morning the day after school let out, I accompanied him to the pet store in town. Rod purchased a dozen tiny white mice and we carefully carried them to his back porch in a wax-lined cardboard box — his mother wouldn't let him bring mice into the house, being even more strict about rodents than insects. I lifted the box top just enough for Rod to slip his hand inside and remove one mouse, quickly shutting the lid tight and placing *Owls of North America* on top. Rod had prepared 3-foot lengths of yellow yarn stolen from his mother's knitting basket, and while he held the struggling mouse, I knotted the string behind its front legs. Alfie watched from his perch just under the porch overhang, his usual daytime spot when he wasn't in the living room digging his claws into the cloth-covered La-Z-Boy and trying to hang on as it rocked.

When the mouse was secure, Rod took the end of the string and dragged the squeaking rodent through the short grass in the back yard while making clucking noises at the owl. The mouse was putting up a fight, trying to run against the string as if it knew its purpose. Alfie hadn't taken his eyes from the action, but when his owl instinct finally kicked in, he swooped off his perch, dove the short distance, and gripped the mouse with one talon. Natural instinct fully took over as he settled back on his perch and tore into the mouse with his sharp beak, consuming it in large, gruesome chunks. The bloody length of string floated to the ground.

"Another mouse!" I cried, as we both ran to the box,

exhilarated. I wanted to watch that awesome spectacle again — I doubted anything this cool would happen at science camp.

Alfie ate four mice during his first hunting lesson. Each time, Rod held the mouse cupped in his hands until he was further away so the owl had to fly longer distances before spotting and apprehending his prey.

It was a triumphant day, and I closed my eyes to replay it over and over in my head as I lay in bed. Before I knew it, I was at camp counting the days until I could come home.

My month at camp wasn't as bad as I thought it would be; I was kept so busy building spewing volcanoes and mini-rockets that I even forgot to keep cursing my parents for sending me away. But on my first day back home in Cardiff, I ran to Rod's house to see my best friend and his owl. The entire family had been at the beach all day; six surfboards were scattered under a tree on the front lawn and the kids were out back playing with Alfie.

"He's catching his own food now!" Rod yelled as he caught sight of me walking through the sliding screen door. "And watch this!" Running at full speed through the yard, then into the brush leading to the foothills, he turned back and whistled. Alfie took flight, his two-foot wings making a soft swooshing sound as they beat the air to gain altitude; he coasted as he approached Rod and made a gentle landing on his shoulder. Rod screamed with joy and scratched Alfie's neck. They walked back to the house together.

"At first he ate mice, then I had to get big rats! Mom hated that! And one day I came out and he was eating a rabbit! He got it all on his own! You should have seen the mess he made! Guts everywhere!"

We sat outside until sunset, telling each other about our summer so far. I had won a couple prizes at camp for my science projects, but they dulled in comparison to Rod's stories — surfing nearly every day from sunrise to sunset, fishing and hunting when there were no waves. He was tanned a deep brown, and next to him I didn't look like I'd ever seen the sun in my life.

"The other baby owls died," he told me, suddenly turning solemn. "They were in the newspaper a couple times after mom dropped them off, but I guess no one had the time to learn how to raise them. I wish we could have kept them all, and Alfie would have playmates. Or you could have had an owl, too."

"My parents would never let me keep an owl. No one is home much anyway."

"Now that Alfie is grown, we don't even need to be home for him, although my mom usually is. He sleeps on the perch my father built on the back porch, and when someone's home we leave the glass door open and he comes inside and hangs out. I found him the other morning curled up with Clancy on his dog bed!" Rod's solemn expression hadn't lasted long; he was back to his normal smiling self, bubbling over with enthusiasm.

After two years with Rod and his family, the Humane Society got word they were keeping an owl as a pet; with five children telling their friends about Alfie, it was surprising it took that long. Alfie had never been in a cage, and by that time he was fully fledged, hunting on his own or following Rod through the trails near the cliffs. The California Department of Fish and Game showed up unannounced one evening to investigate; Rod's parents denied having a caged owl, and after a short conversation and a quick look around the house they left satisfied that they received a false report. If they had looked up, they would have seen Alfie perched near the ceiling in the hallway, another one of his favorite spots, quietly watching them the entire time.

It's been more than 50 years now since Rod rescued Alfie, and although Rod has long since moved away, I still visit with his mother on occasion. Some nights I sit on the back porch with her at sunset and watch the owls swooping through the canyon. Although neither of us is young enough to climb down the cliff face and look, we imagine that Alfie's kids, or his kids' kids, still nest in the same spot, and I like to think that we had a small part in keeping the owls alive in Cardiff.

CHAPTER TWO_

Our lives went on in pretty much the same manner as we finished grade school and entered San Dieguito High School. I still thought of Rod as my best friend, but things began to change for us in our early teens. With a little pressure from my parents, I joined the debate club and the science club, and took the few advanced classes offered; my after-school hours were spent with the other students in these groups, working on projects or slogging through the loads of homework we never seemed to catch up on. Rod loved to read, but had no love for school itself; he spent more and more of his time cutting classes to surf. Some days he'd appear at lunch after surfing since sunrise, some days not at all if the waves were good and the wind stayed light. We always ate lunch together if he showed up to school; otherwise I'd take my place at the table with the other brainy geeks and we'd split whoever's lunches weren't stolen or squashed.

"My parents would kill me if I didn't go to all my classes. They'd probably kill me if I didn't keep straight A's," I

16

remarked one day as Rod moseyed into the cafeteria, his sun-bleached hair still wet from the ocean.

"They had five kids — chances are that one of them wasn't going to be perfect," he joked, his ever-present smile indicating how unconcerned he was with cutting school. "They were hassling me, but I just picked up a sponsor; I'm going to be a competitive surfer!"

That surprised me, since I knew Rod was the least competitive person I had ever met.

"I got two free boards and a few pairs of surf shorts, and really, I never thought I'd stay in school this long anyway. At least I'm doing *something*, so the parents stay off my back. 'It's better than being a bum,' I think was what my dad said."

As my academic pursuits gained me new friends with similar interests, so did Rod's ocean pursuits, and the boys he spent the most time with were not all good influences like me. Occasionally he'd show up to school with eyes more bloodshot than warranted by the stinging salt water, and he was more prone to fits of giggles than normal.

The day we all knew was coming finally arrived when we were 16. Rod simply stopped going to school altogether. He had met a boy with a boat and they started a business fishing and diving for lobster and selling their catch to the local markets. Rod had been diving with his father for years, and by that age he had quite a bit of experience. Many times I'd come home from his house with a gift of squirming, fresh-caught lobsters, which was probably his one saving grace in my parents' eyes besides having a policeman for a father; they never understood why we were friends, and certainly didn't encourage it. They wanted another doctor in the family, and as such, I should only spend time with the "right" crowd. But my mom adored Rod's mom — it was impossible not to

— so I was allowed to continue my weekly visits, whether or not Rod was attending school.

Rod's first business partner was an older boy named Nick, one of his surfing buddies. They made their own lobster traps out of wire mesh and scrap wood and set them out at night, collecting their catch in the morning and taking it to the stores. They quickly became successful, and Rod became the only boy I knew making money at his age — real money, not the pocket change you made stocking grocery shelves or bicycling through town in the early hours before school throwing newspapers on your neighbors' front steps.

A couple weeks in a row I showed up at Rod's house after school when he wasn't home. I knew he was going on a four-day fishing trip with Nick and Stanley, another of his surfing friends, but he should have been back by then. They were headed to San Clemente Island, a 56-square-mile island located 75 miles west of San Diego; the island was owned and operated by the United States Navy since the 1930s, but as early as the 1800s it was a popular drop-off spot for smugglers. When the Navy built an airstrip and commenced military testing, most of the illegal activity ceased, and in the '60s, the island got little use and was for the most part uninhabited. It was a perfect spot for teenage boys to adventure without supervision.

The first time I stopped by, Rod's mom wasn't too worried; he was only a day late, and she assumed he had given her an "estimated" return date; she was used to his obliviousness to schedules. The second time, she was on the verge of panic — his four-day trip was already at 12 days. Since Rod didn't have school to attend and was making his way in the world somewhat responsibly, she realized this feeling of not knowing where he was or what he was doing was something she'd have to get used to, whether she liked it or not. She knew she had lost control of him, and trusted in the good sense she had instilled in him. When he finally came back, 19 days after his departure, he simply told his mother they were having too good a time camping and stayed longer — he always did his best to protect his mother's feelings, even if it entailed a few lies here and there. I got the real story a few days later.

The boys — Rod, Nick, and Stanley — packed five days' worth of supplies on Nick's small sailboat and set out to catch lobster off San Clemente Island; plenty of people caught lobster near Cardiff, so they were looking for a spot they thought would be teeming with enough for a big catch and payoff. Nick's boat wasn't in good shape — a teenager has far too much to do to sit at the dock and fix things — and they barely made it to the island; his solution was to drop off Rod and Stanley, sail home to make the necessary repairs to his tiller and sails, and be back in time to spend the last days of the trip fishing. The boys had a tent loaned to them by Rod's parents and basic living supplies, so they all agreed it was a good idea; it's funny what we considered good ideas when we were teenagers.

Despite the boat's issues, the trip started off well; this was the first time on an extended camping trip without parents for both Rod and Stanley, and they were having the time of their lives. They set the lobster traps, sat around a campfire telling stories and drinking beer, and watched herds of goats roam the island. The goats weren't accustomed to people and wandered close to their tent; the babies trotted along behind the adults on the trails they had made over the years. It was a teenage boy's dream getaway.

On the fifth day, expecting Nick to return at any moment and nearly out of supplies — they had drunk all the beer in the first two days — a storm blew in. The wind howled across the island and rain beat down on their leaking tent. They knew Nick couldn't anchor in such bad weather, if he had started back at all, so they confined themselves to the tent and only ventured outside long enough to refill their water canteens as best they could in the drenching, wind-driven rain. Never fearing for their lives, they finished off the food they had brought while imagining the storm would pass quickly and the boat would arrive the next day.

The thunderstorms lasted eight days. Rod and Stanley ran outside to forage for food when the lightning let up, but didn't find anything edible. They began to brave the tumultuous ocean each day to pull up lobster traps and eat whatever they caught raw; even if the rain let up momentarily, they had no dry firewood. They ate all the lobster from the traps by the third day of the storm, and had nothing to eat for the remaining five days. By the time the storm finally passed, Rod and Stanley were starving.

They had been on the island for 13 days, hadn't eaten for the last five, and when the sun finally broke through the clouds they were overjoyed. Being so young, they only lived in the moment and were sure now that the storm had passed Nick would arrive shortly with spare food and a ride home, so they emerged from the tent to dry off on the shore and wait. It never occurred to them to find a way to collect the puddles of rainwater for any future need, or to reset the lobster traps. Seeing the sun shine down made them happy and the boat was coming, so they lounged in the sand anxiously awaiting Nick's arrival.

They had no idea of the severity of the boat's problems, however, and spent that first glorious post-storm day basking in the sun. Toward evening, when their canteens once again ran dry, they realized their mistake and were forced to look for any remaining water drops on the leaves of the shadier trees, and lick from the nearly evaporated puddles on the ground. They had already packed up the tent that morning, certain of rescue, and when the sun began to set, Rod and Stanley unfolded the wet canvas for another chilly night on the island. They still couldn't start a fire, and they hadn't set out any kindling to dry in the sun.

On their 14th day on the island, the boys were too hungry to think of anything except food. They lapped at the last of the rainwater on the ground and set out to find anything edible they might have overlooked during the storm. They found nothing to eat and sat glumly near the tent watching the goats parade through the camp once again after having sheltered from the storm. An idea formed in Rod's mind.

Nearing sunset, and completely unsuccessful at finding anything else on the island to eat, Rod and Stanley planned their ambush of the goat herd. The goats walked the same path multiple times during the day and had no fear of the boys, and the babies always trailed behind, struggling to keep up. To Rod, it seemed simple to hide behind a tree, grab a goat, and have plenty of food until Nick returned.

As the goats filed past their hiding spot, Rod leapt out from behind the tree and grabbed the last kid's legs while Stanley tackled its body. The rest of the herd scattered in the commotion, and the boys found themselves in possession of a bleating baby goat — their next meal.

They brought the goat back to their campsite, amazed at how such a small creature could put up such a fierce struggle, and more so since the boys were weakened from hunger and barely had the strength to hold on. Its little hooves kicked wildly and raised bruises on their arms and faces before they could fully gain control of its long legs. Using rope from the lobster traps, they fashioned a leash and tied the kid to a tree while they debated over who was going to kill it; killing a

21

crying goat was much different than a lobster or a fish, and the bigger game Rod had experience hunting was always killed from afar with a rifle or a shotgun. Neither boy had brought a knife onshore and all they had on hand was a some- what dull hatchet they had used to chop kindling. The thought of hacking at the goat's neck with a dull hatchet, instead of a clean slice with a sharp blade, made them both feel a little sick. When it was fully dark outside and they hadn't worked up the nerve to kill the goat, they led it inside their tent, fash- ioned a goat bed from their damp towels, and tried to get some sleep.

As morning dawned on their 15th day on the island, and having gotten very little sleep due to the non-stop cries of the goat in their tent, Rod and Stanley woke determined to slaughter the kid and finally eat. They led it outside and again tied it to the tree, but still, even with rumbling bellies, neither boy wanted to kill it. They decided to reset the lobster traps instead, and spent the morning in the now-calm ocean.

While food had been their main priority previously, the blazing sun now put them in search of water. San Clemente Island had a dense population of low-growing, fleshy cacti, and the boys had seen the goats mashing the plants with their horns and licking the juices inside; they decided to give that a try. Using the hatchet, and with a thirst so great he could barely wait, Rod cut a stalk, chopped it open, and began to suck out the juices, not caring if it tasted awful or even if it was poisonous to humans. The reward for his impatience was a painful tongue full of needles, which sent Stanley rolling on the ground with laughter despite his own overwhelming thirst.

While the goat was bleating and straining against its rope and Rod was running in circles with his tongue hanging out, Stanley took his time to properly clean a cactus stalk and quench his thirst. They would have to dissect several stalks for a proper drink, but Stanley had had enough to give his attention to his screaming friend. With nonstop laughter and teasing, he sat and pulled the needles out of Rod's tongue and lips with the pair of rusty pliers they had brought to service the lobster traps. The remainder of that day was spent cleaning cacti — for themselves and their captive goat — and at night the three of them retired to the tent without any sign of the boat.

The bitter cactus pulp went a long way to relieve the boys' thirst, but hunger could no longer be ignored. After keeping the goat in the tent for two nights, and giving up hope of the boat returning, the boys returned to the debate over who should be the one to make the kill. They had become fond of their new pet — although the floor of the tent and all their possessions were now covered in goat droppings — but they couldn't wait any longer. Stanley put forth the argument that he had spent half the day pulling needles out of Rod's mouth, so Rod owed him — and so it was decided. They tied the kid's legs together and Stanley lay across its body. Determined that the goat shouldn't suffer more than was necessary, Rod tried his best for a quick kill but he had to swing the dull hatchet four times to break the tough skin of its neck. They hoisted it off the ground and tied it to a low tree branch to drain away some of the blood.

Stanley collected drier bits of firewood while Rod cleaned the goat, and that evening they gorged themselves on their first meal in days — poorly skinned and barely cooked goat meat.

After a good night's sleep, and with bellies full of leftover goat and cactus juice for breakfast, the boys lazed on the shore, quite pleased with their survival skills. They had temporarily forgotten about their plight, and were surprised to see Nick's boat approaching the island. Seventeen days had passed since they first set foot on the island, and as Nick set the anchor they waded out through the shallows to devour his supply of fresh water and salty snacks. While Rod and Stanley crammed Cheetos and Pop Tarts in their mouths, they collectively decided to stay until the lobster traps were once again full. With no thought of school, or parents who might be wondering where they were, or further storms or starvation, they spent another couple days on San Clemente Island and returned with dozens of lobsters to sell.

It came as a shock to me that Rod felt a genuine sadness at killing the goat; in my mind, it didn't seem much different than the fish or quail he regularly brought home for dinner. I could never have done it, but I've never killed anything in my life. I was barely able to rid my bedroom of a spider in the corner, and usually waited until my dad was home and begged him to do it. But Rod's combination of toughness, sensitivity, and happy-go-lucky adventurousness was what kept him in my life for so many years. Sitting on a hilltop near his house, and in later years in a bar or on his boat, watching the ocean in the distance while Rod told his stories was better than reading *Lord of the Flies* or *Gulliver's Travels* for me. There was no adventure in my life, so I craved his.

CHAPTER THREE_

With nothing but time now that he had dropped out of high school, Rod divided his days between surfing and diving for lobster. Even though I had been slowly granted more freedom as long as my work was done, it was hard to catch up with him; more often than not I'd go to his house and discover he wasn't there. I'd spend an hour talking to his mother, eating home-made cookies and praying to see his sister if she wasn't out surfing before giving up and going home. It wasn't that he didn't want to see me, but his outgoing demeanor and good sales pitches quickly made him more and more business contacts, and keeping up with lobster and fish orders kept him busy. When I did chance to run into him at his house, I was drafted into work — my years of building models and rockets lent me the necessary skills and patience to sit and repair lobster traps while we talked once he'd shown me how it was done. Sometimes Alfie would settle down next to us and watch our work with his keen eyes, as if he was our boss looking out for shoddy craftsmanship.

Rod had been venturing out to the Channel Islands with

Nick to seek out spots which weren't as well-known by other fishermen. The distance was about 150 miles each way, which explained why he wasn't home very often. His need for more and more lobster was due to his newest customer, a group of men who were not as scrupulous about safe business practices as the local merchants.

"I'm working for the mafia," he calmly said, while I spit out the sip of lemonade I had just taken. What normal 16-year-old California boy has mafia connections?

"Aren't you scared? Won't they break your kneecaps if you do something wrong? Are they gonna come after me 'cuz I know about them?" I wasn't a very worldly boy.

Rod laughed. "They just want to buy lobster, that's all."

And that was that to him. No big deal, no worries. It was just another job, and one that paid very well.

He was contracted to provide a certain number of lobsters each week to be shipped to restaurants across the country. His employers didn't require that these lobsters meet the legal requirement of size, a law put in place to ensure an ample population of brood stock to replace what was caught each season. Having grown up appreciating the ocean and learning about the marine ecosystem from his father, Rod understood the ecological soundness of this law and tried to limit his catches to the proper size, throwing back the obviously undersized lobsters. If, when he was pulling lobster from his traps each day, he didn't throw back every one slightly below the limit, it didn't bother him. He didn't think 1/8" was anything to make a fuss over — he had numbers to make for his client. By selling his catch to his east coast connections, as well as locally, he was earning ten times as much money than his father brought home each week.

What does a teenage boy do with so much money? Rod threw parties on the beach. His social circle had grown exponentially since he dropped out of high school; he loved to see people having a good time, and he had the means to provide it, so his reputation, as well as invitations, spread quickly. I was always invited and tried to attend when I wasn't at a debate tournament or falling behind on a term paper. At first I was nervous about going — Cardiff was a small community, and I was never popular. In fact, the first time I went to one of his parties, I nearly turned around when I saw the crowd of kids; right off I spotted four guys who had regularly bullied me through the years, and the popular girls were all wearing extremely intimidating bikinis. The closest I had ever gotten to a bikini was Annette Funicello on television, my nose nearly pressed against the screen, and to be honest, the scantily-clad girls scared me way more than the guys.

Incidentally, I remember an argument my parents had when my dad's *Sports Illustrated* arrived in the mail with the first-ever bikini on the cover a couple years previous — Babette March in her white bikini will be forever ingrained in my memory. My mother argued that it was indecent and should be immediately thrown away, and while my father pretended to agree, I sincerely doubt he respected her wishes.

At his first beach party, I was just about to turn around and walk home when Rod spotted me. He could see I was nervous so he put his arm around my shoulders and walked me through the crowd, introducing me to people I didn't know and making me feel like the party could have been in my honor. A radio blared Top-40 hits from The Beatles, The Monkees and The Turtles, and colorful beach blankets lay spread out on the sand where girls lounged behind sunglasses, looking cool and casually unimpressed as the boys showed off for them. Joints were as plentiful as bikinis, and although I stayed a healthy distance away from both, I had a great time.

Rod wasn't what you'd call a typical "troubled youth."
Even though he had dropped out of high school and partook
of the more common drugs of that time, marijuana and acid,
he appeared to most people a hardworking, respectful boy.
His partner, Nick, was a little more hotheaded, and landed
them in their first serious trouble.

Rod and Nick regularly set lobster traps in the bay near
their home and returned the following day to retrieve their
catch. They kept a log of the locations and numbers of their
traps, and their signature red-and-yellow painted buoys
floated at the surface to mark the exact spots. As the weeks
went by and their success was becoming more widely known,
their homemade traps began to disappear from the water. The
boys dove down, thinking their marker buoys hadn't been
attached properly and the traps were simply lying on the
ocean floor, but they couldn't find any sign of them. As more
and more went missing, they set out at night and pulled up the
traps of the other fishermen in China Cove; they could identify whose they were by the buoys on the surface. They found
their own stolen traps and identified the culprit, a local fisherman who was well known to them. He probably didn't think
twice about stealing from teenage boys — but he should have.

Both boys were understandably upset at the discovery.
Rod dove down to collect their stolen property and was
pondering what words he would have with the man; he
thought a friendly but stern scolding would put an end to the
problem. Nick had other ideas.

They motored around until they located the fisherman's
boat anchored in Mission Bay, just outside San Diego. Nick
kept a shotgun on his boat, which he used if he decided to go
hunting instead of fishing, and while Rod was preparing to
give the man a piece of his mind, Nick retrieved his gun and

proceeded to blow holes under the boat's waterline, yelling curses in between blasts. The man had been sleeping below, and had just enough time to radio the Coast Guard before his boat took on water and began to sink, and he was forced to swim to shore.

At 3 a.m. the police descended upon the bay to apprehend Rod and Nick, who hadn't given any thought to fleeing the scene, but were drinking beer on the boat and laughing as they rehashed the scene of the fisherman jumping into the ocean in his underwear. Divers from the Fish and Game Department were brought in to investigate additional reports of illegal fishing by the boys. Authorities found nearly 3,000 lobster tails in underwater receivers attached to Nick's boat, where they were storing them to bring to shore for delivery that day.

Up until this point, Rod's parents were unaware of the extent of his business activities, but had given up on efforts to persuade him to go back to high school. Their misconceptions about his lifestyle were corrected when a family friend phoned their house at 6 o'clock that morning, advising them to turn on the television — their teenage son was the top story on the local news, pictured in handcuffs and being led away from the docks by police.

The next day, Rod was at home constructing new lobster traps to replace those that were confiscated, pretending to go along with the "grounding" his parents had given him after his father bailed him out. The grounding would only last one day, though, because after so much freedom, he was difficult to rein in.

"What was it like being handcuffed? Did they beat you up when you got to jail? Do you have to go into hiding?" I asked.

"Why would they beat me up?" Rod answered offhand-edly. "They all know my dad anyway. No big deal."

The sum of my knowledge of criminals was limited to what I saw on *The Andy Griffith Show*, sprinkled with the occasional newspaper article on police clashing with Vietnam war protesters. I had virtually no experience with the real world of bad guys, and was prone to let my imagination get away from me. I had envisioned the mafia blowing a hole in the brick jailhouse to spring Rod, or maybe they'd put a hit out on him so he wouldn't rat them out.

When my parents found out Rod had been arrested, and even worse had dropped out of school with no concern for his future, they did their best to keep me from seeing him. They still worked long hours though — my mother especially, since as one of the few female doctors at that time, she always took on more work just to prove she was as capable as the men. I limited my forays to his house, but being told I couldn't do something made it all the more exciting to do it anyway. My determination to remain friends with Rod was the extent of my rebelliousness.

I wanted to attend his upcoming trial; I prepared a short speech citing a real-life lesson in civics to my parents, and was quite surprised when I received permission. While my mother flat out refused to knowingly let me continue to be a part of Rod's life, my father argued that the life lesson involved was what happens to people who flaunt the law — he wanted me to watch the punishment for the crime, and then decide if those were the types of people I wanted to associate with. It seemed like my parents viewed me as a boy teetering on the border of good and evil, even though there was no real proof I was anywhere near going over to the dark side. Their view was most likely due to their spending so much time seeing first-hand the dangers of the world at the hospital, and not spending enough time with me.

The trial began with an inordinate amount of publicity thanks to the Sierra Club's presence. They had heard about the illegal fishing charges — the number of lobsters caught that were smaller than the legal size — and organized protesters outside the courthouse with hand-painted signs calling for Rod's and Nick's hanging, or at least incarceration for a ridiculous amount of time. I sat with Rod's mother, her head bowed in shame, unsure how she could have raised a son who was such a disappointment to her wholesome upbringing.

Because the trial was set several weeks after the offense, a problem with the evidence became clear soon after the opening — no evidence was presented at all. Working in law enforcement in the 1960s was a noble profession, but not rewarded as such. Rod's family itself frequently did without many of life's material comforts. When the bounty of 3,000 lobster tails was seized at the docks during the arrest, investigators took some hasty photos, but the actual lobsters were divvied up between the friends and families of all the departments in San Diego, leaving none to be presented in court. The evidence had been eaten long ago.

The boys were ordered to pay restitution for the damages to the fisherman's boat, which they could easily afford, and lost their fishing licenses for a year. Despite the family's hopes, Rod skated away from his first brush with the law and did not learn the intended lesson.

My parents were equally disappointed, and I was subjected to several weeks of newspaper clippings left on my pillow, describing prison terms for juvenile offenders around the nation. If it had been 20 years later, they probably would have signed me up for *Scared Straight*.

CHAPTER FOUR

I didn't see Rod again for four months after his day in court; he was his same happy self, but thinner and pale, and his sun-bleached hair was much longer than he usually wore it. We were both newly 17 years old, and I had been busily researching colleges and doing the volunteer work my parents had signed me up for at the hospital. I happened upon Rod on my walk home one day, and we greeted each other like long-lost friends; four months is an eternity in adolescence.

"I feel so bad I never said goodbye to you before I had to leave," he told me, always the thoughtful friend.

"It's okay," I replied. "Your mom told me what happened when I stopped by your house. It wasn't your fault."

Rod's parents had watched their youngest son drop out of high school, get arrested, and start hanging out with a dangerous crowd, and it worried them. Punishment hadn't worked, since Rod was making more money than most of the adults he knew at the time and didn't have to rely on his parents for anything. He was still a respectful, nice kid, but beset by examples of the pain and heartbreak other families

32

were dealing with when their kids turned to harder drugs and sometimes overdosed, his parents had to make a tough decision. They sent him away with barely a day's notice.

They told Rod he was going on his first solo surf trip, packed him in the car with his surfboard and backpack, and dropped him off at the Mexican border near Tijuana. As a parting gift they handed him a bus ticket that would take him to the Mexican coast and drove away, tears in their eyes. Still being fairly naive about life, when I found out Rod wouldn't be home for a long time I asked his mom why she thought sending him away was the best decision to turn his life around.

She had looked down at her folded hands on the kitchen table, kept her head bowed as she spoke. "We didn't know what else to do. He's got so many bad influences in his life; maybe getting away from them for a while will make him understand where his life is headed. I don't want to see him die so young."

It was a heart-wrenching decision, but one she thought might save her from the grief she had witnessed other parents endure while planning funerals for their wayward children. But Rod was not like other children.

He looked upon his banishment as a great adventure. He crossed the border into Mexico and cashed in his bus ticket — he wanted to hitchhike. His instantly identifiable good nature quickly got him a ride into the desert, and in Mexicali he got a ride with two men and two women, all surfers, and they took him to Puerto Vallarta in their orange Volkswagen van. For two months they traveled the coast looking for the best waves and slept under palm-thatched palapas in the sand — instead of being punished, Rod was having more fun than he previously thought possible, drinking beer every night, smoking pot all day, and surfing endless sets of waves.

33

One night, Rod was awakened by the girls screaming and jumping around the sand in fright. In a sleepy haze, he thought one of the larger insects had crawled into their sleeping space and he rolled over to squash it with his hand so they could all get back to bed. Instead of the cockroach he expected, it was a scorpion, and it stung Rod's wrist before dying.

The signs of the poisonous venom in his bloodstream appeared almost immediately — pain, then numbness, followed by difficulty breathing. Panicked, the group didn't know what to do; they were near Punta de Mita and a long way from a hospital. They carried Rod into the van and drove to the first set of houses they found, and knocked on doors until a local family finally let them in.

The young surfers brought along the dead scorpion to help Rod; they didn't want his condition to be lost in translation and misdiagnosed. The father took one look at the scorpion as they were carrying Rod onto a pile of blankets hastily thrown in the corner and slashed his fingers in the air across his throat — the international symbol for death. They didn't expect him to live after the scorpion sting, but they were willing to make him as comfortable as they could while they awaited the outcome.

Rod was telling me this story as we walked along the sidewalk toward my house. He was gesticulating wildly. I drank in his story with a thirst I didn't know I had. This was *living*.

"My memories for the next couple weeks are a bit fuzzy," he admitted.

Rod's travel companions left him at the house after spending only one night; they genuinely liked him, but being barely older than him, they had no intention of delaying their travels to care for him. They did the best they could by bringing him to people who would nurse him back to health, then resumed their search for waves.

Rod was feverish and sick from both the venom and the home remedies the family fed him — concoctions like iguana oil mixed with herbs. The family took turns with him, and kept him awake for the first two days of his treatment, telling him he would die if he fell asleep. Gradually, his breathing normalized and the pain lessened, although his arm was paralyzed for two weeks.

He stayed with the Mexican family for a month. As lost as he felt during that time, he never tried to contact his family to let them know he was sick and nearly died; he didn't speak with them for more than three months, until one day he suddenly felt a need to go home. He packed up his few possessions, said a thankful goodbye to his host family, and hitchhiked all the way to Cardiff.

CHAPTER FIVE_

R od resumed his normal activities upon returning home, much to the dismay of his parents. He continued fishing and diving for lobster — without a license now — hanging out with his friends, surfing, and making money. In 1970 he was 18 years old, and bought his first sailboat, a 24-foot wooden, gaff-rigged yawl named "*Wayward*," built in 1928. He partnered on the boat with Stanley, and hungry for more adventures like his trip to Mexico, he began to plan his first ocean crossing. His parents had no idea they had ignited a passion for travel when they left Rod near Tijuana. I doubt that was the outcome they were hoping for.

Excited to show off his purchase, he asked me to accompany him and his mother to the docks where it was tied. Rod hoisted the sails and proudly beamed at us from the deck. The boat was 42 years old and showed its age in peeling green paint and sun-scorched wood, but he was as thrilled as if he had bought a brand-new yacht. It seemed sturdy enough to me, but I barely knew a tugboat from a cruise liner. As we stood alongside admiring his boat, the wind suddenly gusted and ripped the yellowed mainsail from top to bottom — the canvas sails were completely rotten.

"You're going *where*?!" his mother asked incredulously while watching the tatters of the sail flapping in the wind.

He didn't have an exact destination yet, but knew he wanted to travel south, surfing his way along the coast. After finding newer sails and spare parts for the repairs they would most likely need along the way, Rod and Stanley set a date for their departure. They loaded food and water onboard, and finally deciding on Mexico as their destination, they bought the correct charts — although neither knew how to navigate.

Word of their departure spread around town, and more than 50 people, mostly teenagers, arrived at the floating dock to see them off on a foggy morning. A few girls, enchanted with Rod, waved signs and threw flower petals. Rod's family motored out in their small fishing boat to accompany them out of the harbor. As they cast off their lines amid cheering and waving, the dock began to sink from the weight of all the well-wishers; the cheers turned to screams and the crowd scurried back to the main dock when the water rose above their ankles to their shins. Two girls leaning over the edge closest to the boat fell in.

I had begged my parents to let me see Rod off, but I had been scheduled for a volunteer shift at the hospital and they viewed that responsibility as much more important — a lesson that work always takes priority over anything that didn't advance my future career, namely fun.

Someone on the docks had snapped a picture of the sinking crowd on the dock, which ran in the local newspaper the next day.

"Aren't you glad you didn't go?" my mother asked, waving the paper in my face. "You could have drowned."

CHAPTER SIX

The boys set sail on that foggy morning as they watched their friends slowly sinking atop the formerly floating dock. The wind in the harbor was light and progress was slow at first. Rod's family escorted them to the mouth of the harbor on their small fishing boat to say their goodbyes; near the clanging buoys which marked the exit of Point Loma to the open ocean, the fog completely engulfed them and Rod lost sight of his family — it was not quite the farewell everyone expected. He yelled his goodbyes in their general direction, and listened to hear them faintly returned. His family turned back, and Rod and Stanley began their first open-ocean voyage.

Stanley had grown up in a family similar to Rod's, in that they spent time together in the ocean fishing, surfing, and sailing. He had never crossed the open ocean either; the extent of his sailing experience, besides a few trips with Nick, was the family's Laser, a two-person sailboat ideal for teaching children to sail in a calm bay. He had used it to learn the basics, but as a teenager concentrated on fishing and diving.

I wouldn't see Rod in person again for a couple years, but I kept up my regular visits to his house to find out if he had checked in with his mother and listen to stories of where in the world he might be. Rod never told his mother the true extent of his travels, only making the occasional call or sending a letter informing her that he was okay, and she would catch him up on family news. My phone calls from him were much more detailed, although infrequent, and because my life was all work and no play, I looked forward to every one.

Soon after exiting the harbor, the wind picked up and blew off the fog, and the boys sailed south. They had an ancient, second-hand chart but no compass, and had to navigate by dead reckoning — navigation by sight and intuition. They stayed close to shore so they could keep track of their approximate location and look out for potential surf spots; quite often they saw a wave and dropped anchor to spend a few hours surfing. Having no time frame and no specific destination, they were in no hurry. They knew they were heading to Mexico, and that was all the plan they needed.

Three days into their voyage, they were hit by a vicious Northerly storm blowing 65 knot winds — the first storm either boy had encountered while sailing. Rod and Stanley kept their cool, took down the sails, and put their trust in the boat to keep them safe. They had fashioned a sea anchor from an old tire and heavy line for just such an occasion and threw it overboard; the boat still made 6 knots while dragging it behind them. The going was rough; the boys were soaked and frightened, but they didn't capsize as they feared and weathered the storm.

Rod told me some years later that this storm, still one of the worst he's ever been through, was the best learning experience he could have had while starting out his life as an adventurer. It showed him he could survive anything if he believed he could — a great confidence-building lesson that served him well his entire life.

Rod and Stanley came upon a fishing boat near evening while the winds were still raging. The boat was listing heavily to port, and 15 Mexican men wearing life jackets stood on deck, grasping the rails so they wouldn't get pitched off when they collided with a wave, and frantically waving at Stanley and Rod for help. The boys had neither the necessary experience to perform an ocean rescue, nor the space on their 24-foot boat for all the men — there was nothing they could do but stay their course if they wanted to get through the storm safely. The weight of all the men, plus the dangerous storm surge, would surely have sunk their boat. They continued on and hoped the best for the men.

Two days later the boys arrived at Cedros Island off Baja California, and after catching up on much needed sleep while at anchor, they unexpectedly encountered the fishing boat again as it slowly motored into the bay. Despite their apparent need for rescue, they had actually made it safely to land on their own. Rod and Stanley found the entire crew drinking beer in the bar — they had quit their jobs and vowed to never get on that boat again. They were rowdy and drunk, quite understandably after expecting to die just a short time before, and hadn't yet begun to ponder how to find new work on the small island where they were now stranded. The men described how they had shifted the brine — the mixture of saltwater and ice used to preserve the fish — in the hull of the boat to stabilize it, and when the wind subsided they were able to continue landward.

Meanwhile, the captain of that fishing boat was making rounds on the island in hopes of finding a new crew. He approached Rod and Stanley, and offered to teach them how to fish for tuna. The boys were curious not only about learning a valuable new skill, but the thrill of working on a Mexican fishing boat, and went out for an evening with the captain.

After motoring for an hour, they spotted a school of tuna and began dropping nets. Upon pulling them in, Rod saw a number of dolphins caught in the nets as well, as they were hunting the same prey as the tuna. The captain was unconcerned with the by-catch, simply remarking that that was the price of bringing a load of fish to market. The boys were heartbroken at the sight of the dying dolphins, too entangled in the heavy-duty nets to be freed in time to save them, if they could even lift them back into the water with no help from the captain. They declined the job and made haste to get off his boat as soon as they reached shore.

The boys continued with their trip after making some minor repairs to *Wayward*. They rested and refilled their water jugs, bought a few perishable supplies to replenish their stores, and with the weather clear, they were eager to get back to surfing — the entire reason for the journey. Again, they sailed close to shore to spot any waves they might want to try. By drifting along, barely sailing, they did find great surf — mainly waves that only broke when the tide was low. The old navigation chart was updated with excited scribbles so the boys could remember where to stop when they passed by again, along with oceanographic data; without the right tide and swell direction, the spots would not appear to be worth stopping for. They decided to keep the locations a secret, imagining years of sailing back and forth and keeping the empty waves all to themselves.

As they sailed further south, they encountered grey whales breeding outside of Magdalena Bay. It was another fearful experience for an entirely different reason — the whales were aggressive and unpredictable during mating season. The danger, as Stanley saw it, was a male mistaking their boat for a threat and sinking them. Rod thought the greater danger was accidentally colliding with one of the animals and injuring it. With their skills honed from weeks of almost nonstop sailing, they weaved in and out of the surfacing giants until they were further into the bay. After several close calls, they made it safely to anchor in the shallows.

During this stop, a port of entry, the boys were required to get their passports stamped to officially enter Mexico. The town had few buildings, and they easily found the dilapidated and windowless adobe building used as the port authority. They wandered through the few rooms but didn't find anyone inside, just empty desks and dusty piles of books. As they stood at the entry looking around in confusion, a local directed them to the beach — the official in charge of entry was fixing his outboard motor on the sand.

The official, a friendly, toothless old man, led them back to the office and delicately removed a rag-wrapped bundle from the only drawer in his desk. He was grinning excitedly because no one had ever asked for a passport stamp from him before. Rod wondered if they had even needed to bother, but since they had disturbed the man from his work, they figured they may as well make their entry legal.

After adding water to his dried-up ink pad, the man stamped his seal on their passports and charged them $10. He never asked to inspect their boat or what their plans were in his country, only wished them a pleasant stay in Mexico; Rod later learned that customs was not typically so easy.

It was from Magdalena Bay that I received my first letter from Rod. It arrived, battered and stained, nearly two months after he sent it. I was in my first year at UC San Diego — the school my parents had chosen for me as a suitable precursor to medical school. While Rod was now an experienced traveler, I was tasting my very first bit of true freedom living in a dorm an hour away from home. Being away from my parents for the first time didn't have any effect on my lifestyle, though; my course load was intense, even as a freshman, and I volunteered at University Hospital on weekends to better my chances of getting into medical school.

My life's path was chosen for me seemingly from birth, and while it may not have been what I would have picked, I was too far along on that path to figure out what I would have really liked to do — I had no experience with anything else. I'd never been able to withstand the disapproval of my parents, so I studied hard and kept on track to become a doctor. I read Rod's letter dozens of times and dreamed of a life of adventure in the spare moments when I wasn't in study groups or at work in the hospital. After a few letters from Rod, I bought a world map for my wall and used push pins to track the places he visited, destinations I longed to see with him. I saw in my mind palm trees and long, deserted beaches with sparkling white sand; clear water in every shade of blue and a gentle breeze to cool me between dips in the ocean. I promised myself that one day I would see these things for myself, then I reluctantly cracked my books and delved into some part of the human anatomy.

Rod and Stanley stayed in Magdalena Bay for a week, living on the boat moored in 20 feet of water. They surfed nearly all the daylight hours, only stopping to dive for oysters for dinner. The locals were friendly and welcoming, and after the swell dropped they decided to move on; they were sad to leave this first place they had fallen in love with, but the world was calling.

Their next stop was further south at Cabo San Lucas.

Tourism hadn't yet taken hold there, and Rod first saw it as a beautiful beach with only a few simple buildings, including a lone restaurant and bar near the water's edge. Until then, the boys hadn't had much opportunity to spend the money they made from selling lobster and took advantage of the cheap beer and fresh margaritas. They continued to live on their boat and surf with no worries of work or running low on cash.

Although the waves at Cabo San Lucas were almost perfect, the boys moved on once again and sailed 300 miles to San Blas, south of Mazatlan, without incident. There they found a perfect right, a wave nearly a mile long. They also found a number of pretty local girls and soon were spending money without thought, buying drinks and gifts to impress them.

One afternoon while out surfing, the outboard motor from their inflatable dinghy was stolen right off the deck of the boat. It was just a 1-horsepower motor, but valuable to them for transport to the bars at night; they began paddling their surfboards to shore in the evenings to continue wooing girls and getting drunk.

To get to shore they had to paddle through muddy, brown water from the river runoff, with the occasional alligator, but their pursuit of fun outweighed the potential risks of being in the murky water after dark. It didn't occur to Rod why night after night he and Stanley were the only two people in the water so late. The ocean was crowded with both locals and Mexican tourists until sunset, when all water activity ceased, and families packed up their belongings and went home.

One morning, just a few short hours after getting back to the boat from the bar, the boys were awoken by sirens. Curious about the commotion from the large crowd gathered on the beach, they paddled their boards to shore. What they encountered made Rod almost physically sick — two partial bodies lay on the sand, washed up on the incoming tide. A couple had gone swimming in the muddy water after dark; the general consensus of the crowd was a shark attack.

Knowing that I was headed to medical school, Rod thought I would appreciate a full description of the bodies for possible future reference. I didn't, so I'll spare the gory details.

Although shaken at seeing the carnage, Rod and Stanley continued their activities as if they were invincible — nothing seemed too scary after drinking beer and dancing all night, eager to paddle back to the boat to get a few hours sleep before another full day of surfing.

When the swell finally dropped and that perfect right-hand wave disappeared, they knew it was time to move on to their next destination. They hoisted the sail, pulled up the anchor, and entered the clean, clear water outside the bay. Rod was at the helm, but went running to the bow when Stanley spotted a tiger shark cruising alongside the front of their boat.

Rod told me it was at least 20 feet long, but like all fish stories, it may have grown over time. I'm sure it was impressive, nonetheless.

The boys realized for the first time how easily it could have been their bodies washed up on the beach after so many nights paddling while drunk. They thanked God after seeing how close they had come to death, but with the invincibility of youth on their side, the lesson didn't stick with them for long.

From San Blas, the sail to Puerto Vallarta was a short trip. Rod had been there two years previously on his first surf trip and was excited to show Stanley the good surf he remembered before falling ill from the scorpion sting.

Pulling into the bay, they saw a wooden Kettenburg 45

sailboat with several naked women on deck — surfing was immediately forgotten. Possessing an outgoing personality, and being a teenage boy, Rod paddled over to the boat after dropping anchor in the bay. Stanley, of course, was not far behind. The owner of the boat, a well-known counterculture movie star, employed an all-female crew and paid the women very well to work without clothing at all times.

Rod went into great detail once again at this part of his story, and I was a little more pleased with these descriptions than those of the shark attack. I had been dating a fellow biology major at the time (although I still dreamt of Rod's sister and her coconut-smelling skin), but she was shy and I still hadn't seen her completely naked with the lights on.

Rod and Stanley were welcomed on the boat and spent most of their time there, but were warned: "You can party with us, but you can't touch the girls." That was fine with them, though; it was enough to just relax in the warm sunshine with waves gently rocking the boat and drink beer while surrounded by naked women going about their daily tasks.

The women were not merely ornamental. They were the sailors, mechanics and cooks, and did all the work required to keep a large, expensive boat looking its best. This is where Rod's euphemism was born for when he or Stanley needed some alone time below deck on their own boat: "I need to polish the rails." They were young, after all.

Their time aboard the boat was actually quite useful; when the sheer thrill of seeing so many naked women had lessened, they learned celestial navigation from the owner. Rod owned a plastic Davidson sextant, although neither boy owned a watch, so any calculations they could make would only be approximate; the combination of sextant and watch was necessary for complete accuracy. Learning the stars allowed them to sail further from shore without fear of getting hopelessly lost. By day they drank beer and watched the women; by night they drank beer and watched the sky.

While the Kettenburg was in port, the boys had indefinitely postponed further exploration of the Mexican coastline and surfing, and were truly disappointed when the movie star had to weigh anchor to go back to work, taking his naked crew with him. At first, they were almost depressed by losing such great entertainment — both educationally and sexually — but they set out to see the local sights before sailing too far away.

Thus far in their journey, Rod and Stanley hadn't gotten into any real mischief; they surfed, drank beer, and smoked the occasional joint with the locals. In their excitement to make new friends and impress girls by buying them drinks, they were beginning to run low on money, and worldwide networks of ATMs were still over a decade in the future. They had enough money to leisurely sail back home, but considered getting jobs in Mexico if they could find them in order to prolong their trip. They shelved the thought while they surfed, but on a day trip to Yelapa, a short distance from Puerto Vallarta, an opportunity presented itself.

Yelapa is a small fishing village located in the south of one of the world's largest bays, Bahia de Banderas. The pushpin in the world map on my dorm room wall was only an approximate location — Yelapa was way too tiny to be listed.

The town was only accessible by sea, and remains so today without an extreme off-road vehicle. In the early 1970s, very few people visited the village and the locals welcomed the boys and the dollars they spent in the bar.

Soon after their arrival, they met a Mexican man on the beach who offered to sell them marijuana in any amount they desired, from a dime bag to tons of bales; he assumed they had sailed there for that purpose. Rod immediately imagined his next business venture — buying cheap pot in Mexico and selling it for a profit elsewhere. He was excited to get started, although Stanley was a little suspicious of the deal, so Rod gave the go-ahead without asking any questions of the stranger.

In Puerto Vallarta, the boys had refreshed the boat's supplies, mostly eggs, bacon, cheese and cigarettes. With their dinghy motor stolen, they no longer needed to buy gas and decided to spend their remaining cash on marijuana; they imagined they could sell or trade small amounts at a time if they needed to buy anything along the way to their next destination, wherever that might be.

Back on the boat, they rounded up nearly every cent they had and paddled back to shore. They handed $800 to a man they had met just hours before, with only the promise that he'd be back soon.

After two days of waiting impatiently on the beach under a palm tree, afraid to venture far in case the man came to find them, Rod and Stanley had given up hope of seeing their money or the pot. Stanley wasn't as gung-ho about the idea as Rod had been, and spent quite a bit of energy saying "I told you so." They thought they were buying 20 pounds of pot and couldn't understand why it would take so long to be delivered. They could only assume they had been robbed.

Rod had wrapped a 5-pound bag of sugar as best he could to keep it waterproof and paddled it to shore to be used as a measure of weight so they wouldn't get screwed in their deal — he wanted to make certain they got their money's worth. They sat hour after hour with the bag of sugar between them in the sand. They were now certain they had been robbed and were deciding between sailing away completely broke or venturing up the winding, unpaved roads over Yelapa into the town to look for the man who had taken nearly all their money. They were fearful of going after the local man they thought had most likely done this before to other naive tourists looking to score; Rod and Stanley didn't have any friends in that part of Mexico and feared they might not return to their boat if they angrily demanded a refund. With a little persuasion from Rod, they decided to wait one more day before leaving with their lives, and not much else, with no choice but to sail home to California.

On the third day they took up their position on the beach with the bag of sugar, on the spot where they had originally met the man. They waited without hope for most of the morning, and finally getting ready to leave, they saw a small procession of donkeys slowly plodding their way down the winding mountain road. Their curiosity was piqued, momentarily taking their minds from their predicament, and it didn't take long to understand what was happening.

The wind was blowing a steady 15-20 knots, and the smell of marijuana reached them long before the donkeys did. As they slowly approached, tiny flakes of pot wafted down over the boys in the breeze. The small parade of donkeys had homemade burlap sacks tied to their backs; chunks of pot escaped through the holes in the bags on gusts of wind, settling down on the beach.

As he told me the story, Rod recalled the feeling that if he had ever seen snow on Christmas, this is what he imagined it should be like. It was snowing marijuana, and he danced around in it.

Rod and Stanley hadn't been robbed after all — $800 bought them more than they possibly could have dreamed.

The 5-pound bag of sugar, fashioned as a counterweight to ensure they received their money's worth, was abandoned after the man met them on the beach and told them they now owned more than 300 pounds of marijuana. Rod didn't feel he needed to weigh it all, overjoyed at the difference between his initial guesstimate of 20 pounds and the donkey-laden reality he saw before his eyes. The three unloaded the sacks on the edge of the beach just above the water line; the man picketed the donkeys and fetched an outrigger canoe, and three trips were made to transfer the sacks to the 24-foot boat. Rod had no idea he'd bought so much pot, and since it wasn't compressed into airtight blocks, the bulging sacks filled every available space inside the tiny boat's cabin.

After the boat was loaded and the boys were settled back on board, they needed to make a decision: continue on with their surf trip and hope to sell some of the weed along the way, or head back to the States where they knew they could easily sell it all. After a brief discussion of their possibilities, while busily rolling joints to sample their product, Rod and Stanley chose to sail to Hawaii with their contraband. The Big Island was a straight shot west on the prevailing tradewinds, and with their newly learned navigational skills they didn't think they'd get too far off track.

Loaded with marijuana, bacon, eggs, and potatoes, plus their canvas-wrapped 5-pound bag of sugar, they sailed through Bahia de Banderas into the open ocean, bound for Hawaii.

CHAPTER SEVEN

The boys had no idea they'd be sailing with so much marijuana, and it presented a few problems during the next leg of their journey, which were described to me in a rambling — and quite fragrant — letter. Rod had little else to do on this extended leg of the trip but smoke pot and scribble in his spiral-bound notebook.

The rough homemade burlap sacks had quarter-sized holes throughout so chunks of marijuana blew everywhere inside the boat cabin; the smell was nearly overpowering in the confined space. Since the sacks occupied all the available space in the cabin, the only place the boys could sleep was on top of them, and their clothes were constantly covered in marijuana flakes. If they were stopped by the Coast Guard, their arrest would be inevitable — hiding the sight and smell of so much pot was impossible. They had gotten themselves in over their heads, but there was nothing to do except continue with the plan and hope for the best.

Four days out of Yelapa, just past Socorro Island, the wind was a light 3 knots, and the ocean was smooth as glass. They spotted a giant sea turtle swimming along the surface of the water near the boat, which was barely making way. The boys worried they would run out of food well before they reached the Big Island if the wind didn't pick up — fishing hadn't yielded any addition to their meager supplies.

Rod had heard that turtles made "really good eating," but neither boy had ever had the experience, nor had they ever desired to do so. In desperation, they decided to give it a try; it couldn't be any harder than killing and eating the goat. They both recalled how hungry they were while stranded on San Clemente Island and had no intention of starving again, no matter how beautiful the turtle was.

With Stanley steering and Rod keeping sight of the turtle, they slowly approached, expecting at any moment that the turtle would dive below the surface, but it didn't — Rod took that as a sign they were being provided for by nature. He dove into the ocean and swam toward it, and reached out to grab it by the shell. The turtle was completely covered in crusty barnacles, which was likely why it couldn't dive to the safety of the ocean depths. He climbed on top, riding the turtle like a horse, cutting his arms and legs on the razor-sharp crustaceans crowded on the animal's shell and leathery skin. He laid down and tried to paddle it like a surfboard over to the boat, slicing his chest as well. With blood flowing from multiple gashes, Rod began to worry about sharks, remembering the image of the mangled bodies on the beach in San Blas. He was anxious to get back on the boat, but the turtle was too heavy for them to lift up and over the rails.

Using the halyard and a net, the boys winched the turtle up into the air and onto the deck. Stanley went below, walking lightly on the bags of marijuana, to sharpen a knife while Rod began to pry the larger barnacles from the turtle's shell with his fingers. As he waited for Stanley to finish, the turtle began to make mewling sounds, almost like a kitten, and looking closer he saw fluid fill the turtle's eyes.

Having taken a marine biology course on a whim in my second semester at college — and having to reassure my parents that I hadn't decided to become a veterinarian, or indeed anything less than a medical doctor — I knew that turtles have tear ducts. They excrete mucus to rid their eyes of excess salt or sand. Rod didn't know that, though, and he thought the turtle was crying; being completely stoned from all the pot he was smoking made that a logical assumption. He had an instant change of heart about eating the turtle.

Stanley arrived back on deck with the razor-sharp knife and found Rod with his arms wrapped around the turtle and his head resting on its shell — crying as well. Stanley took one look at the pair and dropped the knife; he had a change of heart too.

Together, the boys cleaned the remaining barnacles from the shell and tough skin, said their goodbyes, and gently lowered the turtle back into the ocean. They watched over the side as it calmly swam away, and after a short distance, disappeared under the surface. As they suspected, the massive amount of barnacles had kept the turtle from diving, and they high-fived each other for saving the turtle's life.

With their eyes still on the last spot they had seen the turtle, they heard a thump behind them, followed by a clattering bang, startling them from their dreamy state of goodwill. A malolo, or flying fish, had been spooked by the turtle, and using its wing-like fins to get away, had flown directly into the mainsail and fell into the boat, through the hatch, landing below in the galley. Like something out of a cartoon, the fish was flopping around and banging against a pot — as if preparing itself to be eaten.

"It was karma in action!" Rod had written in his letter. He

believed the turtle had sent them a fish in thanks for sparing its life. It wasn't a big fish, but they ate it and were certain they would have better luck fishing for the rest of the trip.

The Big Island is just shy of 3,500 miles due west from Yelapa. The latitude is 20 degrees, although with a chart and sextant — but no watch to keep time — Rod and Stanley could only estimate their correct heading; they kept watch by day and sighted stars at night to be as certain as possible they were not veering too far north or south. They sailed for a seemingly endless number of days, seeing nothing but more water on the horizon. Their bad luck with fishing had changed and every day they caught at least one fish to add to their dwindling supplies — giving thanks to the turtle every time they hooked one. Rod ticked off the days at sea in his notebook, and both boys began to wonder if they'd ever see land again.

Two weeks into the ocean crossing Rod ran out of cigarettes. Both boys had been smoking joints during the trip, and now Rod smoked them nearly constantly to make up for his lack of tobacco. The weed wasn't great quality but their supply was endless. They sailed through rough seas, doldrums, and near-perfect conditions as the days passed, and after 43 days of being constantly high Rod spotted a snow-capped mountain through his half-closed eyes.

"Fuck, there's snow. How did we miss Hawaii?" he asked Stanley.

The boys rolled on the deck with laughter, assuming they had miscalculated their position and sailed to Japan, and were now staring at Mount Fuji.

"I wonder if they smoke pot in Japan," Stanley remarked.

In reality, the mountain was Mauna Kea on the Big Island — they had kept exactly on course for the entire 43 days — but neither boy realized it snows in Hawaii.

Stanley remembered he had packed an old almanac for the voyage, and after digging it out from under the sacks of marijuana they consulted it to get a better idea of where in Japan they might be, and how best to get back to Hawaii. Looking first at the entries for Japan, they found the approximate coordinates of where they thought they were currently located, and began to plot a course southeast. They knew they had sailed for 43 days, so they estimated they would need to sail back, and a little south, for half that many days again. Tacking the boat, they reversed course and lit up two more joints to celebrate "discovering" Japan.

Thinking he had three more weeks on the boat with nothing to do but smoke pot, Rod decided to read the almanac, forgotten during the months at sea. He paged to the entry on Hawaii to begin to learn about what he thought might be his future temporary home. He knew Hawaii was a group of different islands, but not much else. He had been to Oahu once as a young teenager to visit his older brother who was stationed there for military duty, but had never taken the time to learn anything except where he should hitchhike to find the best surf.

He started with the Big Island since it was the most likely place they'd see from afar. Squinting at the grainy pictures, he noticed snow on the mountain tops and read the passage.

"Stanley!" he called up to the helm. "Turn us around! This *is* Hawaii!"

Excitement was high, as were the boys, as they sailed closer to the Big Island. They had to decide which island they thought would be easiest to offload so much marijuana, and they chose Maui as their destination.

Cruising past the north shore of the Big Island, followed by the east and north shores of Maui, they finally turned west into the Pailolo channel between Maui and Molokai with their sights set on making landfall at Lahaina. As they sailed further south between the islands, hugging the coastline of Maui and with the small town in sight, the wind died. They could see the boats anchored at Lahaina Harbor, but they couldn't reach it without a motor. They hadn't replaced the 1-horsepower engine stolen from their dinghy in San Blas, the current was pushing them out to sea, and they were too far out to drop anchor where they drifted.

They tried to make their way into the harbor for three consecutive days and failed; with no wind, each time they were close the current would pull them back out of the narrow bay, leaving them stranded on the boat within earshot of loud bands playing in the bars. The smells of roasting meat wafted over from the restaurants on the too-light breeze. Rod and Stanley were down to their very last food supplies, and the constant pot smoking made the smells unbearable as they dreamt of all the amazing meals they wanted to eat that didn't consist of fish or moldy cheese. They could only sit on the boat and smoke, praying for wind.

An 82-foot wooden-hulled ketch named *Tattoosh* was the closest boat anchored to where they sat. It was owned by another movie star, and he had been sitting on deck watching the boys try to get into the harbor. On the fourth day of failing to reach Lahaina, the star launched his dinghy and towed them into the shallow waters to anchor. Rod gave him a pound of marijuana for his trouble.

Rod made land on April 23rd, his mother's birthday. He hadn't spoken to her for two months, and his feelings of happiness at arriving unscathed in Hawaii were tinged with a bit of guilt.

Once again, the boys had to resort to using their surf-boards to get to shore — vowing that they would purchase a new dinghy motor when they sold enough marijuana. Their first stop was a restaurant, using the very last of their dollars; it had been more than six weeks since they had eaten food that wasn't prepared on the boat, or made up of anything other than eggs, cheese, fish, or onions. Locating a grocery store, they bought a roll of plastic sandwich bags with the remaining spare change, hoping to make some quick cash selling small amounts of weed. The boys were anxious to party at the bars and make friends, and sample all the local food at the restaurants. As their good luck continued, they found out that marijuana wasn't readily available at that time on Maui despite the great demand; so with their pockets stuffed with baggies of pot, friends and money were easy to come by in the bars that night.

I received a postcard from Lahaina, which actually arrived before the long letter Rod wrote describing the journey. It was the first postcard I had ever gotten in the mail and it was proudly tacked onto my wall, as close to Hawaii as I could pin it without covering anything important on the map. By then, I had told my girlfriend Alicia all about Rod, but she wasn't all that impressed with him and his lifestyle and didn't understand my fascination with him.

Rod and Stanley were invited aboard the movie star's boat to party with him and several women. These women were clothed, somewhat, in tiny bikinis, but the boys still enjoyed watching them — their only company had been each other for so long. Below deck in the massive salon of the boat, a bowl filled with a random assortment of pills sat out on a coffee table, along with a pile of cocaine, for guests to help themselves. Never one to be starstruck, Rod felt right at home smoking joints and conversing with the star while relaxing in his plush lounge chairs. After explaining their situation, Rod secured the use of his dinghy to transport the sacks of marijuana to shore. He had made several contacts in the few days since they had entered Lahaina, and the time had come to offload the majority of their cargo from Yelapa. Rod was a little nervous about the only problem he could foresee: the police station was located directly above the Lahaina Yacht Club, where he would have to dock the dinghy in a slip. He sat and watched a policeman drinking coffee on the balcony, looking out over the harbor, and contemplated creating a diversion across town. Throughout his life his luck had been good, and he didn't know anyone well enough yet to ask them to risk arrest to draw the cops away, so he could only cross his fingers and trust his luck would hold.

Rod and Stanley loaded the burlap sacks into large plastic garbage bags and twist-tied the openings to prevent the overwhelming smell from attracting unwanted attention. They loaded four at a time into the dinghy and covered them with laundry — it was not unusual to see sailors bringing their dirty clothes to shore to wash at the laundromat while they resupplied their boats. Rod drove the dinghy into the slip where he met his contacts, awaiting him in a battered pickup truck parked just a few steps from a police car. They casually offloaded the sacks into the truck, covered them with a tarp, and repeated the process until only one sack remained on the boat. The marijuana was ashore, money was exchanged, and the authorities never suspected a thing. The boys felt a deep sense of relief to be rid of the vast majority of their contraband, and to once again have a ready supply of cash.

Not so long before, when Rod was diving for and selling lobster, he thought he was rich making $5,000 each month, which was indeed a large sum of money back then. At the age of 19, sailing 43 days from Yelapa to Maui with $800 worth of marijuana, Rod and Stanley earned $50,000. Rod instantly knew what he wanted to do with his life — surf, sail the world, and smuggle marijuana from Mexico for income. It seemed like a dream life: doing what he loved and living like a king.

When I received Rod's letter describing all this, I was with Alicia; I thought it would be appropriate to share his adventures by reading the letter out loud to her since she was quickly becoming a major part of my life, and I had still hoped Rod would return to California. Staunchly anti-drug, she wholeheartedly disapproved of Rod's lifestyle and wanted no part of him in our lives. The letter sparked the first real fight we had as a couple, which lasted several days after I flat-out refused to remove the map of Rod's travels from my wall. Looking back, this should have been the first recognizable sign that I was dating my mother, as they say.

CHAPTER EIGHT

A s I was plodding my way toward the end of my first year of college — studying, working, and once a week on Friday nights getting to touch my girlfriend's breasts in the darkened dorm room — Rod was in Maui living his dream: surfing, partying with a movie star and dozens of new friends, and living on a boat in the beautiful, clear blue water offshore of Lahaina. He had no worries about, or plans for, his future, simply living each moment as it happened in his normal happy-go-lucky way. Although he and Stanley had sold the bulk of the marijuana they smuggled from Mexico, and made more money than they ever expected to see at one time in their lives, they had kept a few pounds for themselves and smoked it constantly. Combined with the assorted drugs he was offered by his new friends, which he usually swallowed on the spot, he passed his days in a contented haze.

Rod's first purchases with his share of the money were a rusty, two-tone-green 1956 Volkswagen bus and a couple of scuba tanks. He had never been scuba diving before, but had a basic idea of how it worked; he rigged a hookah-style setup with 200 feet of hose attached to a regulator with the tank strapped on the deck of the boat. He spent hours simply sitting underwater looking around. Rod appreciated ocean life from his years of free diving, first with his father then on his own, but the ability to sit on the bottom for an hour at a time and watch the nearly undisturbed underwater world gave him a whole new perspective.

He and Stanley sailed to Honolua Bay on the northwest tip of Maui to explore and enjoy their carefree days. They took turns using the scuba setup to scrape the bottom of the boat to remove built-up debris, and began to dive again for abalone. The colorful coral was alive with fish, and turtles lazily swam by, unafraid and curious. With no worries about running out of money, the boys did whatever they pleased. Their only pressing need was to refill the tanks when they ran out of compressed air, and since they hadn't thought to bring the Volkswagen to the bay, they hitchhiked a few miles every other day with their empty tanks to the nearest shop.

Sailing back to Lahaina after a couple weeks of quietly enjoying nature, Rod and Stanley met a vacationing drummer from a world-famous rock band and spent several days partying on his boat and teaching his entourage to surf. Rod's outgoing, generous personality made it easy for people of all walks of life to desire his friendship, whether they were multi-millionaires with lavish boats and lifestyles or farm laborers he met at the bars in town.

It was on this star's boat where he ran into Patricia, a woman he had first met in Puerto Vallarta as part of the naked crew; he had spoken with her several times when they first met, but because of the strict No Touching rule, nothing romantic had happened. Patricia had finally left the actor's employment and sailed to Hawaii with a man she had met after Rod had left for Yelapa, but the pair caught lice in

Mexico and she spent the long trip to Maui itching and scratching and miserable. Unable to completely rid herself from the bugs with just the soap she had onboard, she had finally resorted to shaving off her long, thick, dark brown hair and only a short fuzz of new growth covered her head. It took Rod a few moments to recognize her again, and freed from her former employer's restrictions, they quickly became close and began to hang out together constantly, which did not entirely please Stanley.

In a way, Stanley was a bit like me — a little reserved, and not nearly as outgoing as Rod. When Rod began directing most of his attention toward Patricia, Stanley was left by himself and wasn't surrounded with friends, as he had become accustomed to when he was Rod's primary sidekick.

After another few weeks of surfing and partying, and with no plans to sail away for another adventure, Stanley grew bored and homesick, and decided to go back home to California. Rod had no intention of abandoning the wild dream he was living and bought out Stanley's half of the boat, freeing him to fly home with his share of the proceeds from the marijuana sale, and they went their separate ways. It would be years before the once-inseparable friends saw each other again.

Rod sold his Volkswagen and set sail to the island of Lanai at Patricia's urging. Having a new partner in crime, he was ready for a change of scenery and further exploration of the then-remote chain of islands. He was a little homesick as well, but he wasn't ready to interrupt the adventure to visit his family.

Halfway to Lanai, the Hawaiian island eight miles west of Maui, the water was so calm and clear that Rod couldn't resist diving in from the deck of the boat, leaving Patricia at the helm. The wind was light and he was hot from the blazing summer sun, and both were high from sharing a joint; it seemed like the perfect time to hop in the water to refresh. Rod stripped off his surf shorts and tied a rope around his waist; the opposite end of the rope was fastened to the stern so they could continue sailing without fear of leaving him behind. The boat was moving slowly and Rod let himself be dragged naked through the cool water, Maui receding in the distance. He lay on his back and found shapes in the sparse clouds drifting across the blue sky, and thought it was the most perfect moment he had ever lived.

The first stings on his legs brought him sharply out of his pleasant daydream; Rod splashed in the water, scrambling to right himself and looking around to discover why his legs were on fire. They had unknowingly sailed through a group of Portuguese man-of-wars, a creature closely related to jelly-fish, whose thin, venomous tentacles can reach more than 30 feet in length. Rod quickly pulled himself along the rope toward the boat and climbed up the ladder, screaming with pain and covered with nearly see-through, blue-tinted living strings. The man-of-war had wrapped most of his body and stuck barbs into his skin, and welts had already begun to rise. He barely cared about his arms and legs, though — a tentacle had wrapped around the length of his penis, stinging every bit of it; as stoned as he was, he worried he might lose it.

Just when life was going so smoothly — he had a boat and plenty of money, and a beautiful woman to adventure with — losing his penis would be a tragedy of such magnitude from which a young man might not recover. Nightmarish thoughts of never having sex again flashed through his mind as he looked down at his quickly reddening manhood, and all he could do was scream in horror.

Patricia knew she couldn't touch the tentacles with bare hands without getting stung herself, so she went below to search for something to remove them while Rod stood dripping on the deck, staring at his penis and screaming.

Rod and Stanley had never been overly tidy on their voyage, and the interior of the boat hadn't been cleaned since they had purchased it so many months ago; small chunks of marijuana still covered much of the floor. Rod did know where the tools were stashed and shouted directions in between curses and cries of agony. Eventually, Patricia located a pair of rusty pliers in a cupboard — the same pair Stanley had used to remove the cactus spines from Rod's tongue on San Clemente Island, which Rod had never returned to Nick's boat.

Climbing back on deck, she was ordered to peel the barbed tentacles first from his penis. Patricia knelt in front of him and carefully began pulling at the stinging, gelatinous strands, barb by barb, eventually moving on to his arms, legs, and chest. A pile of still-squirming bits of man-of-war was left on the deck while Rod ran his hands all over his body, inspecting it for any remaining. Large, ugly red welts covered him from his neck to his toes, and without much in the way of first aid supplies on the boat, he had to live with the pain until it subsided.

He did have a half-empty bottle of sunscreen, and after Patricia retrieved it, he asked her to apply it to his wounds to see if it would help. When she began rubbing it into his skin, Rod was pleasantly relieved that his favorite appendage did indeed still work properly. He lowered the sails and the couple went below decks just to be certain.

Rod and Patricia spent a month on the island of Lanai, surfing and relaxing on the boat. That island was far less populated than Maui, so they spent much of their time alone, only venturing off the boat to replenish supplies. A free spirit by nature, Rod felt it was time to move on from Patricia after such a short while; he was just having fun, and wasn't interested in being tied down by a relationship at his young age. Patricia didn't want them to go their separate ways, but she didn't have a choice — she could be left on the quiet island to fend for herself, or sail back to Maui with Rod where she already knew many people. She and Rod sailed back, without incident this time, and there they parted, never to see each other again.

"This alone should show you what an awful person he is," my girlfriend had said when we read this part of Rod's letter. "How can he have sex with this woman and then just leave her?"

I didn't agree with her, but knew better than to voice my opinion; Patricia knew what she was getting into when she climbed aboard Rod's boat, just like the other boats before his. She was a few years older than Rod and had been a happy participant in the free love years of the late '60s. In her mind, that way of living hadn't ended simply because she had left California. She made her way through the world and loved whomever she wanted to love, and participated in many great adventures along the way.

I was lucky to be having sex at all — Alicia and I had just started — and only with the somewhat coerced agreement that we would be married in the near future. It took a lot of begging on my part to finally lose my virginity after nearly a year of dates. We progressed from a kiss goodnight to longer kisses, then on to a quick brush of my hand over her shirt, and I thought I was going to explode when I was finally allowed under the shirt. Naturally, when the time came for my pants to come off, I was ready to promise anything, and I did. My parents had only ever dated each other, and I was following in their footsteps in every way.

After leaving Patricia on Maui, Rod sailed back to Lanai

by himself. Being solo didn't bother him at all; in fact he loved it. He was outgoing and charming, and could strike up a conversation with anyone he encountered. He also had several pounds of marijuana left, and since it was harder to find pot on Lanai than it was on Maui, he quickly made friends when he left his boat. One man in particular, Paolo, became an instant companion. He was a world champion archer who had a house on the island, and invited Rod to stay for as long as he wanted.

In the 1920s, the island of Lanai was purchased by James Dole, the president of the Hawaiian Pineapple Company, which later became the Dole Food Company. Most of the 140 square miles of land was used for pineapple production, and with the exception of housing for workers and a few stores, the island was seemingly endless fields. Rod and Paolo spent lazy days driving through pineapple fields in Paolo's WWII jeep shooting pheasant; other days, Rod dove for lobster while Paolo shot venison. They threw parties on the boat and at the house for anyone who wanted to come. Rod loved to be surrounded by people and shower them with food, alcohol and pot, asking nothing in return.

After another month on Lanai with Paolo, the sameness of his days, beautiful though they were, had grown tiresome, and adventure called again. Rod felt the need to explore somewhere new and abruptly sailed away after resupplying his boat.

CHAPTER NINE_

I t was now 1972, and Rod set his sights on Kauai as his next destination. He had memories of a beautiful island with long, sandy beaches and great surf from a short visit with his older brother several years earlier, and was eager to see it again now that he was old enough to enjoy all aspects of it.

His brother had joined the military and was stationed on Oahu in the 1960s; Rod had purchased a round-trip flight from California for $75 to visit him, and took a quick trip to Kauai as well while he was in the islands. That trip was a couple summers before Rod dropped out of high school, and the first time he had dropped acid. Perhaps the turquoise blues of the ocean, the sparkling browns of the sand, and the emerald greens of the trees on the mountains were more vivid in his memory because of the drugs, but he described a paradise I longed to see for myself. I finally did many years later.

Flush with time and money, Rod decided to get to know Kauai this time, to surf the legendary north shore waves, and find the secret surf only accessible by boat. He had purchased a rudimentary map of the islands while on Maui, and chose Kukuiula Harbor on Kauai's south shore as his first stop. Sailing solo between the islands, Rod arrived on Kauai in August as a big summer swell pounded the island's south shore. As he approached the harbor mouth, the waves crashed and broke against his starboard side and he had to sail past them if he wanted to reach the safety of the protected bay. The wind was blowing straight offshore, making it all but impossible to sail through the overhead waves. Because he was sailing solo, his only choices were to brave the surf and risk capsizing or spend days drifting while he waited for the swell to subside.

After several tries — reminiscent of trying to land the boat in Lahaina, only much more dangerous — Rod threw his anchor over the bow. Without the wind in his favor he couldn't get to where he wanted to go, but the harbor was shallow, so he dove into the water after his anchor, clasped it to his chest, and walked along the bottom, slowly pulling his boat along behind him. He walked the bottom a few feet, digging his bare feet into the crevices of the rock for traction, set the hook, and came up for air; he repeated the process over and over for nearly three hours while the waves pounded his small boat. Finally, he made it through the surf and arrived on the island that, unbeknownst to him, was to become his new home.

The harbor had a few homes nearby, but acres of sugar-cane fields dominated the landscape. At the bottom of a hill he spotted a general store, and low on water and exhausted, he paddled his surfboard to the beach with two empty one-gallon water jugs.

The store was originally established to sell everything from food to lightbulbs and personal care items to the sugar-cane workers housed in the area. With his nose pressed up against the glass so he could look in the darkened windows of the closed store, Rod could make out a Mexican taco stand and booths for an interior flea market. Walking behind the store, looking for a water spigot, he came upon a house hidden down a shrub-lined path. Always looking to make new friends, Rod knocked on the door.

"Who the hell is this?" he heard as the door opened a few inches.

The occupant, a few years older than Rod, peeked out into the fading light of the evening and saw a long-haired, scruffy man in a faded t-shirt and surf shorts, grinning from ear to ear.

"Hi. Can I get some water?" the newcomer asked, holding up his water jugs.

Mike was a bit of a loner and loved the privacy of his house. Once he closed the store for the day he was surrounded by sugarcane and quiet, and it suited him perfectly. No one ever came to his door.

Somewhat reluctantly, Mike led Rod behind the house to the spigot where he filled the jugs. They struck up a conversation, and found they were both from California. Eager to keep the conversation going, Rod convinced the man to follow him to the harbor so he could show off his boat, mentioning that he had just arrived hours earlier.

"You sailed *that* from California?" Mike asked incredulously when Rod pointed out his 24-foot boat anchored in the bay. Mike wasn't much of an adventurer, and was instantly impressed.

They sat in the sand on the shore while Rod nonchalantly described his travels, leaving out the illegal parts for the time being. They discovered they shared a love for surfing and spoke of the various waves around the island; Mike surfed daily and knew all the spots. He eventually introduced Rod to Pakalas, a beautiful, long left on the west side.

Neither man would have suspected that this first friendship of Rod's on Kauai would last to this day, more than 40 years and counting.

Sitting on the deck of his boat that first night after Mike had gone back home, Rod was enjoying the new scenery and pondering this next phase of his life. He looked up and saw a moonbow, a rare lunar rainbow. The light from the moon was bright enough to refract on the water droplets in the air, painting a colorful circle in the sky. Completely stoned, Rod understood this to be an omen that he had finally arrived at his destination and should begin to think of Kauai as his home. He had only ever lived with his family in California before and wasn't sure how to begin setting down roots in a new place. He didn't know if he could do it with his still-rampant thirst for adventure, but he felt the need for a home and decided he would try. He envisioned renting a house and finding a job so he wouldn't burn through his hoard of cash. He wouldn't have minded living on his boat forever, but he needed a more secure location to hide so much money, which was stuffed in a pillowcase in *Wayward*'s galley, concealed behind cooking supplies.

He was in no hurry, though, as he sat on the deck of his gently rocking boat and watched the unusual colors fade from the sky.

CHAPTER TEN

R od was content living on his boat in Kukuiula Harbor, surfing the break at the mouth of the harbor when the summer waves were pumping, and meeting other sailors and locals. He wasn't big on research, preferring to live life as it happened, and was shocked when he learned that living on a boat on Kauai was illegal. The harbormaster had seen him a few times, and when he realized Rod had no plans to go anywhere, he forced Rod to leave after a week — threatening to impound his boat if he remained. The nearest harbor with space to dock was Nawili-wili in Lihue, on the east side, so Rod sailed there to look for a place to keep his boat. The only space available was at the cement dock directly under the same harbormaster's office. Since he hadn't yet looked for a house to rent, Rod continued to live on his boat, making sure to avoid the man as much as possible. He continued to live on his boat for several more months without being detected.

Within walking distance of the harbor was a combination restaurant and hotel, just off Kalapaki Beach. The building was the first hotel in the area, but by that time not the only one; at the turn of the century it was Hotel Hayashi, then after renovation in 1929 it was renamed Hotel Kuboyama. The rooms were situated above a family-style restaurant and bar, with a continuous balcony that ran the entire length of the upper floor of the building for the lodgers. When Rod moved to the harbor the bar was called The Oar House, and it became his regular haunt. He hated too much solitude and spent most of his evenings there drinking, meeting people, and evading the harbormaster.

With his quickly dwindling supply of pot and a desire to save the horde of cash hidden in his boat, Rod took a job at The Oar House as a dishwasher. At 20 years old, this was his first legal job; he already had plenty of money and owned a boat, but these were from selling lobster and marijuana. Rod had finally joined the workforce and had taxes deducted from his minimum wage pay like an average citizen. He woke up at sunrise to surf all day, took a quick shower to rinse off the salt, then worked all night scrubbing dishes and bussing tables.

One busy evening a month into his new job, the cook unexpectedly quit. Pops and Blackie, the owners, were in a frenzy; the restaurant was packed, and they asked Rod if he knew how to cook. Cooking had always been one of his passions; he had learned as a young boy in his mother's kitchen and later, prepared most of the meals on camping trips and on the boat. He was immediately promoted from dishwasher to cook, with no other questions asked.

Rod loved his job at The Oar House, the first and last "real" job he would ever have. The dining room had a wooden dinghy repurposed as a salad bar, and he got to know everyone who stopped in — mostly surfers and sailors. He trained a backup cook for the days when the surf was so good he couldn't make it to work; on those days he surfed from sunrise until after sunset. As long as someone competent was in the kitchen, the owners didn't care who it was.

The restaurant had an open kitchen with a massive grill where Rod would cook and chat with anyone who walked by. One summer evening he had nearly 30 steaks sizzling on the grill; the restaurant was at full capacity. He had come straight to work from an eight-hour surf session and was slammed from the moment he walked through the door. As any surfer knows, when you're surfing big waves you will occasionally get tumbled backwards, held underwater, or just get smacked in the face with fast-moving, heavy water; the result, especially after several hours of this, is having salt water in your nasal passages, where it will remain lodged until it loosens up and pours out. The water might stay trapped for hours, but it will always come out eventually.

Leaning over the grill flipping steaks and chatting with a man who had just come in for dinner, Rod's sinuses chose that exact time to expel the water, and out it gushed, all over everyone's dinner. Rod looked up slyly to see if he could get away with it, but the man had been watching and rushed off to the manager to report the unsanitary condition of the food on the grill. Every steak had to be taken off and disposed of, and the grill cleaned, before the man left without even having dinner. Rod was told to get rid of the steaks, but not exactly what to do with them; his friends ate well for the next few days — guys who can't afford to eat steak didn't mind a little saltwater on their food.

After one year of living on his boat on Kauai, and avoiding being kicked out again, Rod rented a house above Nawiliwili Harbor for $125 per month, where he would stay for the next eight years. Kauai was now his home. He sold the boat he had purchased with Stanley for $3,500, the same amount the boys had originally paid for it. The Mexican marijuana he had kept was long gone, but most of the $50,000 remained, and he buried it in several spots in his new yard; none of his friends were aware he had so much money; they only knew him as a pot-smoking surfer who cooked at a restaurant.

Rod did not like buying pot, and now that he had a house, he planted the seeds he had saved and began a large garden on the flat roof. The house was situated on a hill high above the harbor and he was easily able to conceal his activities. His only neighbor was a musician who grew his own pot as well. The downside was that the house was directly under the flight path of the Lihue airport, and he gave a moment's thought about his plants being spotted from the air when they grew into bushes; but as usual, Rod was not worried about being caught. After a few months he had so many plants he began selling the harvest and bringing in an additional $2,000 each month, most of which he saved and added to the stash buried in the yard.

Besides his cooking duties at The Oar House, Rod was in charge of cleaning the ducts and hoods in the kitchen, sort of a chimney sweep for grease to ensure it didn't build up and clog the ventilation or catch fire. Always industrious, and not afraid of hard work, he saw this as another business opportunity. After getting the hang of this dirty and much-hated task, he approached other restaurants on the island and got himself hired for the cleaning job no one else wanted to do; it was work he could perform at night when the restaurants were closed and he couldn't surf. This turned into a new business, Kauai Hoods, and he even printed up business cards depicting himself with a machine gun. He worked for cash, and could fall back on this new work as the reason why he always seemed to have so much money all the time if anyone asked. He hadn't made plans for another smuggling run to Mexico yet, but saw more of them in his future and didn't want to do anything suspicious that might call attention to him or his roof-top garden.

Rod worked alone after the restaurants were closed. On a night he was cleaning ducts in the cafe at the Wailua Golf Course, he climbed up his ladder and began scrubbing as usual. Working his way further and further into the duct, he pushed his shoulders past a tight squeeze and became wedged in, unable to move forward or backward. It was nearing 3 o'clock in the morning, and all the lights in the restaurant were on, unusual for that time of night. A police car pulled in after seeing the lights, and assumed it was a robbery.

The cop peered into the windows and saw Rod's ladder, but not his legs sticking out of the duct, and entered with his gun drawn. Looking around and not finding anyone inside, he cautiously called out and heard Rod's muffled reply coming from the ceiling, legs kicking furiously to make some noise to aid in his discovery.

After assessing the situation and finding no robbery taking place, only a crazy guy stuck in the ceiling, the cop stood on the ladder and slowly began pulling Rod out of the vent. By then covered in grease, he slid out fairly easily with the cop's help.

Rod never intended for Kauai Hoods to be a successful business, but as a young man everything he seemed to do made him more money than he had ever imagined as a boy from a blue-collar family. Between cooking, cleaning vents, and selling the pot he grew, Rod was making thousands of dollars each month. He surfed most days, and worked most nights, existing on just a few hours of sleep. He loved his life.

CHAPTER ELEVEN

I n 1976 I was entering my final year of medical school and planning a wedding. Well, I wasn't, so much as Alicia was, with the expectation of getting married and starting a family as soon as I graduated and started my residency. She had taken a job as a high school biology teacher after getting her bachelor's degree and was living in a house with two other female teachers until we could move in together — after the wedding, of course.

We had another of our Rod arguments about whether he would be invited to the wedding. After reading his letters about selling pot and sleeping with women he had no intention of marrying, Alicia wanted nothing to do with him. She had never met him, but imagined that he was some sort of satanic creature who would instantly corrupt me and convince me to dump her to lead a life of wickedness. I pointed out the fact that I grew up with him and still made it to medical school without falling victim to his evil ways, but at one Sunday dinner with my parents she recruited them to her cause and that was that. My best friend, my hero, the man I secretly wished I could have been, was not invited to my wedding.

Overruled, and quite honestly more upset about the matter than I let my family know, I asked if I could invite Rod's mother, with whom I still kept in touch. She occasionally sent me boxes of cookies while I was an undergrad, with notes updating me on the happenings of her family. This request was denied as well.

The most upsetting aspect of the entire matter was that not one of them actually knew Rod. He was the most generous person I'd ever met, and so outgoing and happy that everyone who took the time to get to know him loved him. All Alicia had to tell my parents was "he sells marijuana," and he was forever branded as a bad person. I tried to explain that he only did it so he could afford to surf every day, but that only made it worse.

After Rod's next phone call, I stopped sharing his stories. If they mistakenly thought he was bad before, I wasn't about to try justifying his next life choices — they were better off not knowing any of it.

In the early 1970s, cocaine was making a comeback as a recreational drug for the wealthy; it was a party favor for those who could afford it, and was sensationalized in movies and television. The price of cocaine was high enough that people of average income were not able to afford it, so it hadn't begun to destroy families or cause addicts to lose their jobs and homes. It would be 10 years before cheaper crack cocaine was introduced and wreaked havoc in lower-income neighborhoods of major cities.

While my fiancé was drawing up our guest list for the wedding and picking out her color scheme for dresses and flowers, Rod received a visit from an old surfing buddy from Los Angeles. He had flown out to Kauai for the great surf, and to test the waters of a possible new market for his product. He had come through the airports, whose methods of security were quite relaxed compared to today's standards, with a quarter pound of cocaine strapped under his shirt. Rod happily accepted the gift, seemingly given in exchange for lodging at Rod's house and a tour of the best surf spots. The cocaine market on Kauai was almost nonexistent at the time, and Rod easily found willing buyers, local professionals like bankers and real estate agents, who could afford it and used it to attract new business opportunities at the parties they threw.

The demand grew exponentially, as it always does for addictive substances, and soon Rod had a network throughout the islands and was turning four kilos a month, a profit of about $60,000 for him. Everyone was having fun; no one — yet — was losing everything they worked for to pay for their addiction, and Rod threw more wild parties at his house. None of his friends knew of his connection to the influx of cocaine on Kauai, and he preferred it that way.

With a steady income, more than he could possibly spend, he quit his job at The Oar House to surf more and enjoy life. He disappeared from the island once a month, first to Los Angeles to meet his supplier, then eventually to Mexico and South America to procure his supply directly from the source, cheaper and of better quality.

With more money, mostly added to the stash buried in his backyard, and more free time came more adventure, but now closer to home. At the time, a 100-foot tower stood above Nawiliwili Harbor, used for loading raw sugar onto barges destined for refineries on the mainland. Rod's house stood on the hill above the tower, and at parties they'd stare at it and dare each other to jump off into the deep water below. One night, after a day of surfing Cannons on the north shore, drinking tequila and snorting coke, they decided to try.

Big wave surfers are daredevils by nature, and with the addition of some drug-fueled courage, Rod and a friend climbed the rusty metal rungs of the tower. This friend, James, was also an adventurer, and had introduced Rod to hang-gliding over the Napali Coast, jumping off at Koke`e State Park and landing on Kalalau Beach, a drop of nearly 4,000 feet alongside jagged cliffs and forests to the sandy edge of the ocean.

Falling 100 feet into flat water is almost like landing on concrete if you don't enter streamlined. The first time they attempted the jump from the tower — after finishing off the baggie of coke they brought to the top to ensure they didn't lose their bravado and climb back down — James went first; instead of clamping his feet together, he left them slightly apart and the shock of the impact left him painfully swollen and unable to walk, and barely able to pee, for several days. He floated at the base of the tower in agony, shouting "Keep it tight!" up to Rod. He didn't want to let Rod know how badly he hurt himself and wanted him to jump, too. Rod made his jump and landed in good form, pumped with coke and adrenaline and ready to go again, until he realized he had to help James walk back to the house. He got James an icepack for his bruised crotch and they drank tequila until the high wore off.

They were young and carefree, and after James recovered, they jumped again and again. They never could convince anyone else to join them after hearing the story of James' injury, which Rod told over and over to get laughs from his friends.

CHAPTER TWELVE_

I n 1978, Rod's sister paid him a visit on Kauai; she had become a real estate agent — although I would always picture her as the flat-chested young goddess in a bathing suit and cutoffs from our pre-teen days and not the business-suited professional he described — and after touring around the island to see what the market was like, announced to him that she had found the perfect house for him to buy; she was one of the few people who knew Rod had the money for a house, and where it came from. He hadn't been looking to buy a house, content in the $125 per month rental he had been living in, but she persuaded him to accompany her for a look. He went along to humor her, with no intention of buying or moving.

They drove to Kapaa, and Rod fell in love the moment they pulled into the driveway. The two-story house had a wrap-around ocean-view lanai and he walked directly to the rocking chair facing the water, sat down, put his feet up on the railing, and announced he'd take it without even entering to look at the interior. He envisioned it as his new headquarters — plenty of land and privacy to grow marijuana and throw amazing parties — and promptly went home to dig up his hoard of money to buy it with cash. He still had plenty of money left, and after quickly closing on the house and moving in his few possessions, began to bury the remaining plastic-wrapped cash in his new backyard.

With grand visions, Rod recruited friends to help him build a second house on the property, which was zoned for three separate rental units. He never actually rented them out, but kept them as furnished places where anyone could stay when visiting him on the island. Or, more often, for friends to sleep off all-night alcohol and cocaine binges.

I had the opportunity to stay there once, and it took the most eloquent argument I've ever made in my life. I had graduated from medical school and accepted a cardiology residency at University Hospital, happy to remain close to family and friends, and at a place that was already very familiar. Alicia, now my wife of two weeks, was ready to start our own family, and asked what sort of wedding gift I'd like before our lives got crazy with a new career and little ones running around our house. I asked for a few days to visit Rod, and finally see a small piece of Hawaii. Surprisingly, she said yes — on the condition that she accompany me; the trip would also serve as the honeymoon we hadn't made plans for since we weren't certain where I would begin my career.

I called Rod, excited to let him know we were coming.

"Great, buddy! I can't wait to see you again; it's been too long. I have a cozy little apartment you and the wife can stay in. Congratulations on the wedding, by the way. I can't wait to meet Alicia!"

I had never told Rod that Alicia did not approve of him — she flat-out disliked him — and spending time with him was not high on her list of things to do on Kauai.

"She can't wait to meet you, too," I lied, "but she has

quite an itinerary set for us. I'll probably only be able to get away for one evening."

"After six years living here, I know all the places to see. Why don't you let me play tour guide for you? We have so much to catch up on."

"I'll run that by her," I said, already knowing her answer. "But for right now, let's plan one evening and I'll get away so we can really talk. She won't mind if I disappear for a few hours."

Rod gave me a specific date for the following week that I should be at his house, along with his address. "I have a few friends stopping by that you should meet; we'll sit around and drink some beers. Sound good?"

I agreed and we hung up. He hadn't clarified that "a few friends stopping by" meant a bachelor party he was hosting, which in retrospect was for the best because I wasn't a very good liar and would never have been allowed to attend.

Our impromptu honeymoon was wonderful, and for the first few days we saw all the sights of Kauai from our rental car. Neither Alicia nor I were very sporty so we drove to lookout points and snapped pictures instead of hiking, but we snorkeled and had romantic dinners and conceived our first child.

The evening we had set aside for my visit to Rod arrived, and I kissed my wife goodbye, telling her I'd be home before too late. I had booked her an appointment for a manicure and facial at the spa of our hotel, and she was content to be on her own getting pampered, even with her reservations about my spending time with such a dubious character.

When I pulled into Rod's driveway I knew the evening was not going to happen exactly as he had let on. Besides Rod's F-150 in the driveway, a dozen other cars were parked in various spots on the lawn and on the street, with more pulling up as I stood looking around. Rod spotted me from the front lanai and hurried down to bowl me over with a giant bear hug.

"Aloha!" he greeted me. "It is *so* good to see you!" He hugged me again, rocking me from side to side. He reminded me, in that moment, of a giant, shaggy, happy puppy.

It was, indeed, good to see Rod again after all the years we'd been writing and talking on the phone. Despite the loud music of the band set up on the far side the house and the people milling about with drinks in hand, I still had tears in my eyes. I was reconnecting with my best friend from childhood and the sense of nostalgia was almost overwhelming. Nearly everything I had learned in life that wasn't from school had come from Rod, and that made him more than a friend to me — he was a teacher of things I couldn't manage to see for myself.

Our sentimental greeting was interrupted when a battered white van pulled into the driveway and drove across the lawn to park at the front door, horn blaring as the scraggly, bearded driver shouted, "They're here! They're here!" out the open front window, through which he dangled a half-finished beer.

Rod grabbed me by the arm and pulled me in their direction. "Oh boy, do I have a surprise for you! Come meet James and his friends!"

Approaching the van, I smelled pungent marijuana smoke wafting out as the panel door opened, but that didn't shock me as much as what I saw. One by one, women exited the van, and it was the first time it occurred to me that I hadn't seen a single other woman anywhere around the house. Each was wearing a long, tan-colored overcoat and spiky high heels, and they were all different nationalities — white, black, tan, brown, every shade of beautiful woman, all painted in excessive makeup.

When they were all standing outside the van and the shared joint was back in James' other hand, he said, "Okay, ladies, let's make our entrance."

On cue, they untied their belts and dramatically threw the coats to the ground. My eyes nearly popped out of my head.

"Hookers?" I turned to Rod and asked, although I only glanced away for a moment because I didn't want to miss a move they made.

"Dancers," he replied with his giant grin. "James just picked them up from the airport. I flew them in from Oahu — we don't have any strip clubs here."

He reached over to touch my chin, indicating that I should close my gaping mouth.

"You need a drink," he said, and I agreed, but couldn't get my feet to follow him toward the house.

The women began their parade to the front door, and again as if on cue, the band struck up a quick-tempo song unlike the mellow Hawaiian music they had previously been playing. High-heeled legs began stepping in time, and sequined, barely covered buttocks started shaking. Hoots and hollers sounded from everywhere as men poured from the interior of the house and lined the porch to watch the procession. My feet started working, but only after Rod grabbed my shirt sleeve and tugged. I followed, entranced.

"I thought you'd like this," Rod said, and walked next to me, appreciating the women in front of us as much as I was.

I later found out that this was the third of five bachelor parties he had hosted at his house that year, and planned this one when he found out I would be visiting since I didn't have one before my wedding. Another was his own, as he had recently married a woman he had been dating for a few years, but whom I had never met. With no close neighbors and a never-ending supply of marijuana and cocaine, he was known for throwing legendary parties and needed only a moment's notice to spread the word and have dozens of people show up. It reminded me of the parties Rod used to have on the beach as a teenager; he hadn't changed a bit, and everyone still wanted to be his friend.

The night was crazier than I could have imagined, and in my nervousness about being so close to strippers I drank more beers than I ever had in one night. I began to walk through the house looking for a phone in a quiet place so I could call my wife and let her know I had to spend the night — I had not been able to pass up the shots of tequila in honor of my marriage, nor the beers, and driving was no longer a possibility, even if I had been foolish enough to try.

The women were scattered throughout the house dancing, or so I thought, and the first closed door I opened as I searched for a phone taught me not to open any more doors without knocking. Two men were hunched over a table snorting lines of coke while a third was getting a not-very private, but very intimate, very nude lap dance. I was stunned, and froze in the doorway as I witnessed a scene I had never pictured in my wildest fantasies.

Looking up, one of the men invited me to join them "for a bump," and if I had a few extra dollars I could get my own private dance. I declined, and slowly backed out the door and closed it behind me.

After I recovered my wits, I went in search of Rod to ask where I might find a quiet phone extension and he led me to an alcove on the second floor that wasn't quite quiet, but was at least not surrounded by illicit activities. I called Alicia at the hotel and woke her up after she'd been pampered into an early bedtime.

"What do you mean, you're not coming back tonight?" she asked.

"I've had a bit too much to drink and can't drive. Rod has an extra bed and I'll get back early tomorrow, I promise. And we can do whatever you want to do," I slurred in response, holding onto the wall to keep from falling over.

The band struck up a fast new song and the shouting became almost deafening — the strippers must have started a new routine, and I couldn't hide the noise from my wife.

"Are you at a bar?" she asked. "I thought you were going to his house to have dinner and catch up on old times." I could hear the disapproval and mistrust in her now-awake voice.

"Well," I lamely began, and stopped. I was in no condition to think through any plausible explanation for the men now shouting "Show us your tits!" and prayed the phone line would garble the words as I hurried to cover the mouthpiece.

"Listen," I began again. "I drank too much and think I'm going to be sick. I gotta go." And I hung up the phone. I knew I was in a world of trouble, so I decided to enjoy the rest of the night.

Chaos had broken out everywhere in the house, and I cracked another can of beer and settled myself on the end of the couch to quietly observe. Somehow, in the midst of cocaine-fueled naked women and crazed men throwing fistfuls of dollar bills, I fell asleep. When I awoke, the sun was starting to rise and I was covered with a quilt. Rod was making coffee nearby, whistling a happy tune. Bits of sequined clothing and g-strings littered the floor, but no one else was in sight.

"Hey, sleeping beauty. Did you have fun last night?" Rod asked when he noticed my bleary, half-open eyes.

He handed me a steaming cup of black coffee and led me to a rocking chair on the lanai to watch the shades of pink and orange spread over the ocean.

"I knew you probably had to leave early so I haven't been to bed."

I sipped the coffee to get rid of the fuzz coating my tongue. My head hurt. "You really haven't changed a bit, have you?" I asked.

"Why should I?" he answered. "I love my life."

CHAPTER THIRTEEN

W hen our first child was born, I was deep into my first year as a doctor, and Alicia left her teaching job to be a full-time mother. We had purchased a modest three-bedroom house, and I painted the nursery three separate times to accommodate Alicia's changing intuition of what sex our child would be. We were well on our way to becoming a stereotypical suburban family. On my days off, which were seldom, I mowed the lawn and walked to the park with Alicia to show off our baby boy to the families of the teachers and doctors we knew. Mostly, though, I just worked at the hospital, arriving home to find our son already asleep and my dinner reheating in the oven.

Some months later I received a package in the mail; it was battered and postmarked long ago, and I immediately knew it was from Rod. It contained a colorful, hand-made Mexican baby blanket; Alicia took one look and promptly packed it away in the attic.

"It smells like horses," she said.

Rod had been on another business trip to Mexico and took the time during his busy days to pick out and mail a baby gift.

He flew to either Mexico or Colombia once a month to purchase uncut cocaine; while waiting for his purchase, he went to appliance stores and bought cheap stoves or refrigerators, whatever was readily available, and had them delivered to the docks. His plan was to stuff the bundles of coke in the appliances before they were loaded on the barge, and at first he wasn't sure how to do it. He walked the docks during the day to see where he would have to go, never once being questioned about his business there. When he returned at night with a gym bag stuffed with cocaine he encountered two security guards at the gated entrance; they were lounging on chairs playing cards on a small metal folding table, smoking cigarettes. A single bulb was the only light shining from above.

Taking a deep breath and gathering his courage, he approached the men and spoke in Spanish.

"Good evening," he began with as close to an innocent smile as he could. "I have a shipment leaving tomorrow morning and I forgot to pack these gifts. Can I put them in my boxes?"

He held out his hand to shake, with two $20 bills palmed.

"Do you know where your boxes are?" the security guard asked. He stood and shook Rod's hand, pocketing the money.

"Yes, thank you. I'll just be a moment."

Rod walked through the gate and stopped a few feet inside; from his bag he took out a knife, packing tape, and a flashlight. He located his boxes, sliced them open, and taped the kilos of cocaine inside the appliances. When he was satisfied they couldn't be seen in a casual inspection, he carefully resealed the boxes to look like they had never been opened.

On his way out, he stopped at the guard station once again. It would have been easy enough to walk past, say good night, and make a successful getaway, but it was never Rod's nature to encounter people without a few minutes of chat. He spotted a third chair nearby and pulled it up to the table. He took out his pack of Marlboros and offered a cigarette to each man, which they accepted.

They smoked and talked for an hour, and Rod gained two valuable new friends in Mexico. On subsequent trips, he brought two cartons of Marlboros and two bottles of tequila, as well as a cash bribe, and he was allowed to come and go on the docks at night whenever he wanted, with thanks from the guards. He spent a few hundred dollars to bring in $75,000 of product.

Returning home, a previous months' shipment would have arrived, and he loaded the appliances onto his F150, removed the contraband, and gave the appliances to any of his friends who needed them. I'm not sure what people thought about Rod always having stoves or refrigerators to give away, but no one complained about his generosity or questioned their origin.

By importing cocaine and the harvest of the large garden of pot plants at his house, Rod was able to spend three solid weeks each month surfing. Unlike the guys who could only surf before or after work, or a couple hours on days off before family time, Rod could and did regularly spend each day from sunrise to sunset in the water chasing big waves. He travelled the island and paddled out wherever it was pumping, spending many winter days at Cannons on the north shore and summer days at Pakalas or Acid Drops to the south. He knew everyone in the water, and spent just as much time splashing and talking story as he did riding the waves. Rod knew everyone wherever he surfed, and they all wanted to talk to him and find out the date of his next party as he paddled back out to the break.

Rod wasn't looking for business connections as he

chatted his way through the ocean. He simply loved having friends, and would throw parties just to invite new people he met. Everyone had a unique story to tell, which he was genuinely interested in hearing.

The parties at his house resembled music festivals; kegs of beer lined the walkways, and multiple bands played throughout the day — he only hired strippers for special occasions. He made everyone feel welcome and completely at home in a crowd of strangers. Besides being a world-class surfer, his greatest gift might have been his ability to be a friend to every type, nationality, and class of person he ever met.

CHAPTER FOURTEEN

I was home alone on a rare day off when Rod unexpectedly showed up at my front door. Alicia was at the pediatrician's office with Nicholas, both for a one-year checkup and a pregnancy exam; we suspected our second child was on the way. I was never so relieved that she was away from home as when I opened the door to see him, looking like he hadn't slept in days. He was thinner than I'd remembered, but with the same happy grin on his face. As I heated up leftovers for him and brewed another pot of coffee, Rod told me about his latest adventure before he had to continue on to visit with his mother.

He had had a problem with his cocaine suppliers overseas so he traveled to Manhattan Beach, a coastal community about an hour southwest of Los Angeles, to make a purchase. He had a huge network of buyers and didn't want to let them down, even though the quality wasn't as good. He had stayed at a rental house with Joe, another old friend from his surfing days in California he had kept in touch with over the years. Joe had Quaaludes and tequila, and Rod came over with five kilos of coke; they broke open a package to test it out, envisioning a pleasant evening of listening to music and talking story.

A little after midnight, with music blaring from the record player and no possible chance of getting to sleep any time soon, blazing white lights suddenly lit up every window in the house as if daylight had dawned while neither man had noticed. Rod's brain was coated in a drug-induced fog, but he had the sense to dive to the ground, pulling Joe with him. They crawled to the nearest window and stealthily peeked through the curtains. The street outside was crowded with police cars, lights flashing, and armed officers laying across the vehicles with guns drawn and pointing at their house.

Rod sat down on the floor under the window, back against the wall. Panic set in, and sweat poured down his face. If he had been followed from his pick-up, the cops would have been there much earlier; he assumed the man he had bought the coke from had given him up in return for a lighter sentence.

"Come out with your hands up!" bellowed throughout the house. The police must have known he was inside, and with the music at full volume, they could hardly pretend they weren't home. Joe was a little quicker on the uptake, possibly having taken fewer Quaaludes than Rod, or maybe he had just done more coke, and he sprang into action. He grabbed the remaining Quaaludes from the coffee table and crawled to the bathroom to flush them down the toilet, screaming "Rod, you have to run for it!"

Cocaine was everywhere, split into lines on the table, spilled on the floor, and wrapped in small bricks piled up with Rod's belongings. They couldn't possibly clean it up or flush it all before the cops smashed through the door.

Rod crawled on his belly up the stairs and into a bedroom at the back of the house. He stared out into the backyard at a large oak tree with branches extending to just a few feet away from the window, and weighed the choices in his mind. Assuming the worst, he could stay and get busted with most of five kilos of cocaine and all the other assorted drugs Joe was busily trying to flush away; that would put an end to his happy-go-lucky life as he knew it. Or he could open the window and dare a jump to the nearest branch, pray it held his weight and try to make his getaway.

With the thought of jail time, and probably quite a bit of it based on the amount of coke in the house, Rod had just made up his mind to escape when a group of policemen entered the backyard, fully surrounding the house. He was trapped. He dropped down to the floor so he wouldn't be seen through the window, then crawled on his belly back down the stairs to consult with Joe.

More demands of "Come out with your hands up" came through a loudspeaker outside, but no action was taken to break down the door. Joe turned down the music slightly so they could hear if windows were broken anywhere in the house. Rod began snorting more coke to clear the Quaalude haze from his brain; it might give him an edge if he had to run, but it also might be his last drug binge for a long time, so why not?

The siege lasted nearly two hours. Neither man could understand why no move was made to enter the house, so they lay on the floor doing lines, shaking in terror, and awaiting their doom. They had nowhere to run.

A change in sounds came to them from the front yard — people shouting, men moving, doors slamming. Rod was certain the cops had waited long enough for them to surrender and were given the order to bust into the house. Rod and Joe snorted a final line each in preparation for what would surely be the worst moment of their lives, and crawled to the window to see what was going on.

What they saw completely baffled them.

A large man was walking cautiously toward the line of flashing police cars, hands in the air. When he got within 10 feet of them, he was tackled by the nearest officers, who then beat him with their clubs. In their drug-addled confusion, they forgot they were supposed to be hiding and stood up in front of the window to get a better look.

Having subdued the mysterious man, the police threw him into the back of the nearest car and they all began to pack up and drive away. Rod and Joe sunk to the floor, completely shaken, and not at all understanding what had just happened. When the last of the cars had left, leaving only a news van outside, Joe turned the music back up and poured them fresh drinks.

"What the fuck just happened?" Rod wondered aloud.

"I wish I hadn't flushed all the Quaaludes," Joe answered.

They laughed nervously and sat in the relative quiet, sipping their drinks. Then, since there didn't seem to be any consequences to their actions of the evening, they split another small pile of coke into lines with a credit card.

Neither man could sleep that night, both from the anxiety of their near-bust and the large amount of cocaine they had ingested. At 6 a.m., Rod turned on the local news; the top story was of an armed burglar being chased through a residential neighborhood and taking refuge under a house — the same one Joe was renting. The police had no idea Rod was hiding five kilos of cocaine inside.

At the end of the news story, the video from the street showed the man crawling out from under the house; Rod and Joe could be seen clearly standing in the window, scared out of their wits.

I had been wondering why Rod looked so haggard, and that explained it.

"I haven't slept in three days," he told me, "and it took me two more days to convince myself it was safe to leave the house."

"You could always give up your gangster life if you want to sleep better at night," I told him.

He only laughed, and began to clear our breakfast dishes. He had to get to his mother's house, and more importantly, leave my house before Alicia returned and saw the state he was in. I desperately wanted them to be friends, but that was not the day.

"Travel safely," I said as he walked out the door.

CHAPTER FIFTEEN_

W hile he was still on a high from getting away with his latest adventures, Rod was approached by an old friend with a business proposal. This friend, Robby, was a sailor and smuggler as well, and the two had met on Kauai through mutual friends. Rod was now certain he was bulletproof — that he could do anything he wanted and not get caught. It wasn't so much that he vocalized that idea, but it had become an ingrained part of his mentality — so long as he remained a kind, generous man, and took care of his friends and family and loved his life, things would continue to go his way. He believed in karma and his nature was to be good to the people surrounding him, so why should anything go wrong?

Rod and Robby flew to Australia, where Rod bought a 70-foot steel-hulled ketch named *Old Salt*. He used cash and a false name for the purchase because the sole purpose of the boat was smuggling. The plan was to sail to North Vietnam to meet a waiting freighter; they would load 80 tons of hash onboard from the ship and deliver it to a buyer in Seattle. It was a risky trip, more so than anything Rod had yet attempted. He didn't need the money, but he was restless for a different kind of adventure.

Rod and Robby took on a small crew in Australia, Chester and Craig, to help them get the boat ready for the trip and take shifts standing watch at night while they were under way. They told the men they were delivering the boat to a new owner in Canada, but didn't mention the contraband they would be carrying. If they had any objections about the haul, it would be too late at that point to do anything about it; they were getting paid very well for their services, and Rod didn't foresee any problems — he was completely unable to imagine anything going wrong.

The crew left Australia and headed northwest toward their destination through the Makassar Strait through Indonesia, between Borneo and New Guinea. Robby thought of himself as a prankster and filled some of the long hours on the water thinking of jokes he could play on his fellow crew members. He had once set a drunk friend adrift in a dinghy with no motor at night in the ocean — it was only funny because they found him safe in the morning, passed out and stuck on a protruding reef.

Rod was in charge of the cooking, as usual, and had stocked the boat with plenty of fresh fruits and vegetables along with the normal staples of bacon, eggs, potatoes and onions — foods that would keep longer. During the early stages of the trip he made elaborate, colorful salads to use up the quickly perishable items, and hopefully prevent food boredom when they were left with only the basics. They didn't have refrigeration and their supply of ice would melt long before they reached their destination.

One evening, Rod had prepared a salad for the team; lettuce, tomato, red and yellow peppers, mushrooms, onions, carrots, beets, and sunflower seeds. He turned to retrieve bowls from the overhead cabinet in the galley and Robby snuck up behind him, tipping the large wooden bowl and its contents over his head. Sliced vegetables and dressing tumbled down Rod's head and shoulders to the floor; the bowl sat on his head like an oversized hat while Rod stood frozen in disbelief. Robby howled with laughter and ran off to tell Chester and Craig about his joke, but Rod didn't think much of it.

A few nights later, around 2 a.m., Rod was standing watch and noticed multiple blips on the radar screen closing in on the boat from different directions. He ran below to wake Robby, telling him they were being surrounded, and what he suspected. They woke the others and unpacked the weapons they had brought onboard, purchased in Australia in case they ran into trouble in the more remote areas through which they had to sail. They had two hunting rifles, a double-barreled shotgun, one semi-automatic pistol, and four 9 mm pistols.

Rod switched on all the boat's lights as the fast, nearly silent zodiacs approached, and Rod's crew opened fire in four different directions. Gunfire was returned, thankfully not striking any of the crew or anything of importance on the boat. After a few tense minutes of bullets whizzing past them from the dark while they took cover, the pirates broke off and fled; they had lost the element of surprise and were not willing to board a boat with armed men already firing at them. This incident was Rod's only experience with pirates in his sailing career, which would eventually cover nearly the entire world. It left the crew severely shaken, but alive and unhurt, and it added to Rod's notion of truly being bulletproof.

Approaching the South China Sea, and now not too far from their meeting with the freighter, the weather had begun to turn foul. Rod was at the helm, exhausted from several hours of night watch in gusting wind and rain; he had taken an extra watch so the rest of the crew could catch up on sleep in case they needed all hands on deck. Robby came to relieve him and Rod headed below to his cabin. The next thing he knew, Robby was waking him up for his next watch — he felt awful, like he hadn't slept at all.

Rod made coffee and donned his foul-weather gear again, still soaked, and headed for the helm. When he arrived, Robby was laughing hysterically at the bedraggled figure of Rod, yelling "Just kidding!" In reality, Rod had only been asleep for about 10 minutes, but Robby was getting the hang of practical jokes. Rod was so happy to go back to bed he wasn't even mad.

Far into the South China Sea and 300 miles from the freighter, they received word of an incoming typhoon, which explained the increasing winds. Now within sight of the Philippines, Rod wanted to turn and wait out the storm in a sheltered port if they could find one, but let himself be persuaded by Robby to stay on track and outrun the storm to get to the freighter on time.

The storm was Typhoon Warren, and the winds reached 135 miles per hour; eventually it killed a total of 18 people and left thousands homeless throughout the region. It was the worst storm any of the men had ever seen.

The winds generated waves with 40-foot faces, and time after time, Old Salt reached the top and slid sideways down into the trough, submerging almost the entire 70-foot steel hull. If the boat were to be held underwater for too long it might implode from the pressure, and that was a real and terrifying concern for the men as they were tossed about in the waist-deep water inside. Rod had learned years ago from his boyhood open-ocean sailing adventures to trust the boat, and he kept a calm demeanor despite how scared he actually was.

The men had dropped the sails long ago at the first sign of sustained high winds, and were at the mercy of nature for nearly 18 hours as the typhoon raged around them — they hadn't stood a chance at outrunning it. They took turns at the helm, exhausted with the effort of trying to guide the boat to stave off disaster. They tied themselves to the rails to prevent tumbling overboard when the boat lurched in a wave. Two men were required to hold a course to prevent them from turning sideways in the rolling and breaking waves, but due to high winds and spraying water in the pilot room, it was nearly impossible to breathe. Robby stumbled below, retrieving masks and snorkels to wear on deck while they struggled to save the boat and their lives.

The crashing of the boat had thrown open the cabinets in the galley, sending the contents to smash against the walls and float in the rising water inside. Shards of broken glass from dishes and alcohol bottles were floating everywhere. Forks and spoons and food drifted into the cabins.

Craig had been brought on as a crew member with very little sailing experience, but eagerly joined so he could learn from the veteran sailors, Rod and Robby. The typhoon was more than he could handle, though, and he panicked to the point of losing his ability to think clearly. Instead of leaving the steering to the men who knew more and could choose the path that had a chance to save them, he barged into the pilot room and tried to take control. Using the superhuman strength of someone fighting for survival — and scared out of his mind — Craig wrenched the wheel and tried to turn the boat around, thinking if they could just go back the way they had come, they would be safe. But as every sailor knows, in a severe storm you have to take the course that leads toward survival, which is not necessarily the direction you want to go. Rod threw Craig to the ground while Robby regained the helm; Craig staggered below to his bunk, partially underwater, to pray — probably the best job he could be assigned with the danger they faced.

The boat continued to rise and fall on waves as high as a five-story building, barely making it over the crests before slamming into the troughs and submerging, tossing the men about the boat as if they weighed nothing at all. Chester, Rod, and Robby fought at the helm as best they could to keep the boat pointed in the safest direction; they were past exhaustion and running on fear. Craig returned to the helm, crazed, and tried again to take control. He became more physical, punching the other men to force them to relinquish, as he mistakenly thought he knew the way to safety. Rod had a passing desire to throw him overboard so he wouldn't kill them all.

Rod retained his common sense, however, and dragged Craig below instead of committing an act his conscience would not permit. The men struggled and were thrown about, but he eventually got Craig to his cabin and locked him in, leaving a snorkel in case the water got too high.

With Craig out of the way, they had one less problem to deal with as the wind raged and the boat nearly capsized again and again. Rod returned to the helm and asked, "How much worse can this get?"

He should've known better than to tempt fate with such a question.

The black night was terrifying to the crew as they rode out the typhoon, barely able to see the sea in front of them — the white of the breaking surf appearing before them just as it broke on the bow, sparkling terribly in the boat's lights. The wind blew the stinging salt spray sideways, so the men continued to wear snorkels and masks to breathe. Lightning, a sailor's worst nightmare, flashed over the seas for hours until finally striking Old Salt with an ear-splitting crack. The bolt hit the steel-hulled boat and shook it as they rode the waves. Blue flames raged back and forth in the rigging, and the men let go of the wheel for fear of being electrocuted. The boat was lit up like a Christmas tree, but the rain drenched the fires before they could do more damage to the furled sails or deck.

When the flames finally dispersed, Robby yelled at Rod, "Don't *ever* say that again! Things can always get worse!"

The strike fried most of the boat's wiring and electronics, but miraculously, the engine kept running. The lightning melted holes in the aluminum mast and the shroud lines snapped, weakened from the lightning. The steel cables twanged and echoed as they whipped across the boat and lashed the steel hull. The electronic navigation was gone, and as the hours passed and the storm lessened, Rod and Robby reckoned their course as best they could from their charts, not entirely certain where they were although they could see land. The boat was severely hobbled and they had no idea how to find the freighter, if it was even still waiting for them. The men took turns resting.

They could finally make out the lights of Hong Kong's skyline in the distance and pointed the disabled boat toward them. Without navigation there was no point trying to find the freighter and its cargo of hash; they had been blown so far off course it would take them days to get to the meeting spot, but since Typhoon Warren had wreaked havoc on the entire South China Sea, the freighter was probably long gone. Rod went in search of Robby for his watch to let him know of the change in plans — to limp into port at Hong Kong and recover from their harrowing ordeal. Craig was still hiding in his cabin, afraid to come out to face the consequences of punching his fellow crew members in a time of crisis; Chester was working on deck, trying to patch the shroud lines so they could use the weakening wind to get to port. No one had any idea where Robby was.

Rod searched the 70-foot boat, walking through every passage and opening every door, but he couldn't find Robby. He alerted Chester, alarmed, and they began to panic, thinking Robby had gotten careless as the typhoon waned and had been swept overboard when no one was watching. They frantically searched the boat again, calling out loudly, but still Robby was nowhere to be found. The trip could only have been worse if everyone had died — Robby was gone, the boat was nearly destroyed, and the money-making cargo was lost. He sat on deck with his head in his hands, devastated and close to tears.

Until the giggling reached his ears.

Looking up, he saw Robby's head peeking through a port-hole in the deck, his eyes wet from laughing so hard.

As Rod and Chester had searched the boat, Robby had been a step ahead of them the entire time, shimmying up through hatches and diving under sails as either man approached. He had kept this up until he couldn't contain his laughter anymore. Robby felt it was his best practical joke yet.

Despite seeing the lights of Hong Kong, it still took three days to reach the harbor. The engine was still running, but barely, and Chester had been unable to patch the shroud lines with the materials they had onboard so they could only fly the smaller, damaged mizzen. All they wanted to do was get off the boat and into a bar for a drink — or six. The supply of booze they packed was gone; the bottles they hadn't drunk before the storm had been shattered by it. They wanted to drink to celebrate their survival and forget their close call with death. They spent the next days manually pumping the last of the water from below, salvaging food and cleaning up the mess inside the boat.

Robby was the first to jump off the boat when they finally tied up at the dock in Hong Kong.

"I'll be back as soon as I can," he called over his shoulder as he ran down the pier. He hadn't said where he was going, and Rod was annoyed that he just left when there was so much work to be done.

Craig was kicked off the boat immediately after Robby left. Rod handed him his pay for the trip, even though he himself would not be paid, and he caught a taxi to the airport to fly home. He was never invited back on a boat with any of the men.

Chester and Rod were securing the boat and getting ready to look for a bar when Robby returned. Although he had never been to Hong Kong, it had taken him less than an hour to change money, find a liquor store, and return with three cases of beer on a small cart — he had a natural instinct for finding mischief, which served them well at that time. The three men sat on deck drinking, taking in the sights of the city from the deck of Old Salt, and toasting their survival.

Drinking as much beer as fast as they could, they soon grew restless. At first, they were simply content to be alive and sit in the peaceful harbor waters, but they had all been on the boat too long and needed to get on land. They also needed to get away from each other for a little while; emotions had been running high for too long, and with no real privacy on the boat they each needed some space.

Because they had missed their rendezvous with the shipment of hash, Rod only had $5,000 on hand, which thankfully had not been washed away when *Old Salt* took on water. He gave Robby and Chester $2,000 each and they departed for town, only to return to the boat a few days later after they spent their money on booze and women.

Rod needed to get away as well and rented a hotel room in town. He explored the city and happened upon Club Volvo, an underground gentleman's club. As he walked down the stairs, hundreds of women dressed in their best finery greeted him. The bar was as big as a city block and featured a convertible Mercedes on a track; he was invited to climb in and take an automated tour of the women.

Although Rod was married, the marriage had not gone well from the start. He was too much of a free spirit and was off on business trips too often. She was too fond of what he brought home from those trips, and grew increasingly dependent on other, more dangerous products he didn't bring home. He was expecting to get divorced when he returned and no longer cared to be constrained by his relationship. He just wanted to let off some steam after the harrowing trip through Typhoon Warren.

Rod was quite taken with one of the first women he had seen as he entered the club, but wanted to experience the ride in the Mercedes through the immense underground room. Being an intensely social person, he also wanted to meet as many people as possible on his first trip to Hong Kong. He rode in the backseat of the otherwise-empty convertible past smiling and waving women. The car was on a track and had no driver, and slowly wound its way past tables, either empty or with other customers chatting with women. By pressing a button, a flag was raised and the car stopped, almost like when riding on a city bus. Any time a woman looked interesting to him, Rod raised the flag, stopped at a table, and bought drinks. He climbed back into the car to continue on his tour, stopping frequently and unaware he was being charged at every stop simply for speaking with women.

At the end of the track — two hours later — he had met several lovely women but couldn't get the first woman he had seen out of his head, a beautiful lady of Chinese-Thai ancestry. He disembarked and led her by the hand to the madam of the house to arrange for his purchase, pulling out his wallet. He left the boat with $1,000 — and it wasn't nearly enough to cover his trip in the Mercedes and the handful of drinks he had bought.

His bar bill was $100, and each time he had stopped the car to chat incurred an extra $100 charge, even though he hadn't had sex with any of the women. He was presented with a bill of $1,300, even before he took his chosen woman back to his hotel room. Rod considered, for just a moment, making a run for it, but the club had large, unfriendly looking bouncers placed at even intervals throughout the room, and he couldn't imagine getting past one of them, much less several, and certainly not with his companion. He chose to put it all on his credit card instead.

Rod took his new friend back to his hotel room, where she ended up staying with him for two weeks, not the one night he had planned. They mostly stayed in the room ordering room service, or tried to avoid his crew members when they wandered through the city at night. Their room overlooked the harbor and Rod could see Old Salt, but he didn't let Robby or Chester know where he was. He needed some time away after the experiences of the pirates and the typhoon; time to relax and not worry about anything.

Eventually, though, he realized he needed to get home; he'd been gone for almost nine months, first to purchase and make ready the boat in Australia, and then the trip to Hong Kong and his subsequent vacation from real life. When he brought his companion back to Club Volvo, he was charged an additional $3,000 on his credit card; he tried to negotiate it down, but didn't have any luck.

With clear weather most of the way, and having made many repairs while in port, Rod, Robby, and Chester sailed back to Australia where Rod dropped off his crew and sold the boat. When he finally called to check in on his wife, she asked him about the several thousand dollars of charges at the club, the hotel, and restaurants. Being acquainted with many sailors throughout her life, she had no doubt as to what the payments were for — a man simply does not spend that much money on other men. This was her impetus to begin divorce proceedings against Rod, although it was an amicable separation; unknown to him, she had been seeing another man for several months whom she would eventually marry.

After parting company, Robby got in touch with Rod from Australia. The buyers who had hired them to make the run into the South China Sea had also hired a second boat for the same purpose, leaving from a different location. The other boat had avoided the typhoon and made the rendezvous with the freighter, successfully delivering the tons of hash to Seattle. Whether Rod's boat would have taken on the shipment had they made it, or were hired as a decoy to lure patrol boats away from the other, remained unknown, but he never received any payment — it was just another adventure for Rod.

CHAPTER SIXTEEN_

After speaking to Rod at length on the phone — he was excited to tell me about Hong Kong and narrowly escaping death a couple times — I decided I wouldn't relate any of his latest adventure to Alicia. She was still nursing our second child, a girl we named Lucy, and wouldn't be amused at his exploits.

I had been vehemently against the name — the only girl I knew of named Lucy was from the Peanuts comic strip, always fooling Charlie Brown into failing to kick a football. But Alicia won out, as she always won every argument we had, stating that after carrying a child for nine months and taking care of our toddler while keeping house, she should be awarded certain privileges such as the final say on a name we couldn't agree on.

I was the one who went to work each day, sometimes for 12 or 16 hour shifts, and provided my family with everything they needed or wanted. That fact was never given consideration though, and the one time I ventured to disagree with the childbirth argument left me sleeping on the couch for a week, much like Snoopy on his doghouse.

Rod was safely back on Kauai from Asia and Australia, and had decided to work from home for a while, with the occasional trip to Mexico. He had permanently split from his wife and had built a 14-person redwood hot tub to ensure he was never without companionship, although he was the type of guy who would have dozens of visitors even if he lived in a shack. People just loved him.

His family visited often; his brother and sisters brought their children to meet Uncle Rod, always their favorite. Rod had just finished converting part of his wrap-around lanai into a growing area for marijuana when his oldest sister and her son arrived on Kauai. He needed the extra space to keep up with demand for his product. While his sister was getting some much-needed vacation time by herself on the beach, Rod enlisted his seven-year-old nephew to help start his new crop. No one in the family thought of marijuana as a bad thing, not like the harder drugs, but even so, Rod didn't tell his nephew what exactly they were planting.

With seeds purchased on one of his trips to Mexico, he filled 100 Styrofoam cups with soil and his nephew followed behind him dropping a seed in each and adding water. Together, they arranged the new garden in a sunny spot while Rod explained the basics of growing plants, loving the time he got to spend with the boy.

Rod had quit smoking pot, along with all the other drugs he used to enjoy, but that didn't stop him from continuing to grow or import them for sale. He had begun to see the harm caused by cocaine, and with the introduction of even more destructive crack, wanted to find a way to make his marijuana growing more profitable and eliminate his importation of coke entirely.

In 1981, Kauai was still a quiet island, only beginning to truly get discovered by tourists, and the local population was still less than 40,000. With the vast majority of the residents living on the outer edge of the island, most of the 552 square miles was empty, rugged wilderness used by hikers and hunters. With jagged cliffs of extinct volcanoes rising over a mile above the ocean, only the hardiest of adventurers followed the pig trails or scaled the rocks to glimpse the most remote areas.

Looking for a large plot of land to increase his marijuana production, and in a place that was difficult to access and couldn't be linked to him, Rod began scouting the mountains. He hadn't done much hiking since he was a boy in the mountains of Cardiff-by-the-Sea, but he was still in great shape for his 30s, and so donned his hiking boots, packed a tent and some essentials in his backpack, and began making trips into the interior. He hiked from Waimea on the west side, all over the Waimea Canyon, and found many great open spaces, but without nearby water. A stream was essential for his operation. He hiked the north shore, and after several weeks and many trips, thought he had come across the perfect spot.

Rod chartered a helicopter to view the entire area from above before he committed himself to his new project. Flying high above Kalalea near Anahola on the island's northeast side, a small plateau came into view; water flowed in streams from the rainfall and the area was nearly inaccessible by land. Rod made up his mind as he had the pilot hover above — this was the spot.

His seedlings, now numbering in the hundreds, were growing quickly on his porch as he began collecting the necessary supplies for the massive undertaking he envisioned. His first major purchase was a Bell 206 Jet Ranger helicopter; he would have to make multiple supply dumps on the mountain and couldn't risk exposure from a pilot he didn't personally hire. Rod interviewed pilots, telling him very little of his real plan, only that he was an explorer and needed to be dropped off with supplies on a regular basis. The first three men he found wouldn't take the job; flying in high winds close to the mountain's peak was dangerous and they were happy to continue with their jobs as regular tour guides. The fourth man he interviewed — call sign Mr. Personality in contrast to his gruff, nearly silent demeanor — had been a helicopter pilot in the Vietnam War and wasn't scared off by anything Rod described as his potential duties. He had done his share of drug-running on the mainland and had no moral problem with Rod's plan, and his paycheck would be large enough to ensure he kept quiet. Not that he spoke more than necessary to answer Rod's questions.

Since Rod wouldn't be using the helicopter very often, he found partners to chip in to cover the huge expense and keep the pilot busy. His share was $25,000 of the $225,000 machine, which was used frequently by his partners to take visiting friends on private sightseeing tours of the island. No one except Mr. Personality knew what Rod was using his air time for, and Rod paid him extra to keep the interior clean so as not to give away his project.

Having a helicopter didn't make the undertaking easy; it was simply a way to drop heavy supplies at the growing site. The first drop on the mountain consisted of long lengths of heavy rope and tools to create hidden lines to cross gullies, climb the cliffs and cross rougher terrain so Rod could hike in when he needed to. With the pilot hovering just above the treetops, unable to land on the plateau, Rod dropped the bundles in the center of the site then climbed down a knotted rope before jumping a few feet to the ground. It took him a week of camping in the wilderness to finish this first stage of the project before he hiked out to his waiting truck.

The second drop contained boxes of PVC pipe and more

camping supplies. These Rod loaded into a net and left in his truck in an open field. The pilot landed nearby and hooked the net, by rope, to the belly hook of the helicopter. While hovering above the site, he released the hook and the entire load fell to the ground. Rod constructed an irrigation system to siphon water directly from the streams, flowing downhill into increasingly smaller branching pipes to consistently water the entire grow operation. The third and fourth drops were bales of soil, rakes, and shovels to create his garden. With carefully packed marijuana seedlings on the fifth drop, Rod began to plant the mountaintop, shifting the bulk of his production away from his house.

With camping supplies and nonperishable foods left at the site, Rod only needed to carry clean water with him when he hiked in to observe the growth of the plants. It took a great deal of effort to hike from the base, even with his carefully constructed rope lines, but he loved nature and the hard work it took to reach his destination. He frequently spent a week at a time in solitude on the mountain, tending his garden, reading a book and enjoying the spectacular view.

He prearranged drops of fertilizer with the pilot every month while he was on the mountain. Waiting below, the pilot lowered burlap bags of granules that Rod opened and spread around his plants. After each drop he had to hike out with the net for the next use.

His favorite time to be on the mountain was during a full moon. He didn't need to use his lantern to make his way at night, and the light glistening off the rolling ocean waves was mesmerizing. Out of sight of buildings or city lights he felt close to nature, second only to when he was floating out in the ocean on a surfboard, orchestrating his movements with the flow of the waves.

On one full-moon evening after a fertilizer drop, Rod was

sitting by his tent enjoying the slow crackle of his campfire when a herd of wild pigs burst into his garden. The pigs normally had copious amounts of wild fruit to eat and didn't bother Rod's plants, but the scent of the fertilizer in the breeze attracted them; they gouged open the bags with pointed tusks and began eating as fast as they could. Worried more about his plants than his own safety — wild pigs are fierce and can weigh hundreds of pounds — Rod spent the night banging pots and pans together to chase them away. When they grew accustomed to the noise he ran after them brandishing flaming branches from his fire, swinging wildly and yelling to keep them from charging at him. The thriving garden, nearing a time of harvest, was torn up from the hooves of the animals and it took Rod days to repair the damage and salvage the plants. He left the fertilizer off to the side, unspread, until he could get to town to purchase fencing materials and drop them to the site a few days later. When he returned by helicopter, the fertilizer was completely consumed and he erected a barrier so the pigs couldn't return to ravish the garden.

The helicopter couldn't land at the site, but Rod hiked in one day with a plan to get picked up from the mountaintop, something he had not yet attempted. He had bought a 120-foot climbing rope and tied knots near the bottom for hand-holds, and arranged a date and time with Mr. Personality to meet him. With a growing knowledge of the wind speed and pattern at that altitude, it seemed like something they could easily accomplish and perhaps do more often when Rod harvested more and more marijuana at more frequent intervals.

He didn't think to discuss further plans with Mr. Personality for the first pickup, and assumed the pilot would fly him to the closest spot he could land, where Rod would climb into the helicopter and complete the trip down the mountain buckled comfortably in a seat. When the aircraft neared, Rod strapped on a backpack stuffed with the first ripe buds and waited for the rope. Because a helicopter pilot cannot take his hands from the controls for more than a quick moment without risk of losing control, Mr. Personality had rigged a quick-release knot holding the coiled rope by the open door; he tugged it to set the rope free, and with a deft dip to the left side, the rope slid out between the cabin and the skids, secured to the seatbelt harness inside. The swirling wind caused Rod to dance around trying to catch the rope, and when he did, he tied a knot around his foot and grabbed hold, preparing for a short flight.

His pilot had his own idea in mind for the pickup, and Rod found himself hanging on with all his strength as he was flown at 80 miles per hour — sometimes over a mile-high drop, other times barely clearing the treetops — spinning out of control. The pilot meant to take him all the way to the base of the mountain before setting him down.

The force of the wind ripped the backpack from his shoulders, causing Rod to lose his grip with one hand and nearly losing hold completely. The strap of the pack had come off one arm and was secured only around the other elbow, propelling him into wider spins as his center of gravity shifted further out, and he couldn't move, frozen in place with one hand grasping and one foot tied onto the rope. He thought he might throw up.

Terrified about falling, he threw his open arm as hard as he could toward the rope and regained a second grip as the helicopter descended the mountain at high speed. Finally back to Anahola, his truck in sight, the pilot set Rod down then landed nearby. Rod lay on the ground, his backpack an uncomfortable lump beneath him, sputtering curses; the ride was the longest 10 minutes of his life. Adrenaline spiked throughout his body and he sat up, shaking. Mr. Personality sauntered over, pleased with their first successful pickup from the mountain; he didn't understand why Rod was so upset. After taking several minutes to pick himself up off the ground, Rod drove home and spent the rest of the day soothing his nerves with vodka-cranberry cocktails.

The next logical purchase was a harness if he was going to get picked up again — Rod never wanted to repeat the experience he had had dangling off the end of the rope, unsure if he could hold on. He needed to visit his plants, but didn't have the time necessary to hike in and out. He found a harness similar to a bosun's chair used for climbing boat masts. He modified the climbing rope to tie the harness to the end, and made several more knots along the length; the pilot would have to fly a few feet lower to pick him up but he had plenty of clearance above the treetops on the plateau where the garden was located.

The pair flew out to the site and Rod lowered himself down the rope as the helicopter hovered above. After a few minutes of checking the welfare of his plants and making a mental list of what was needed the next time he came to work, it was time to depart. Rod couldn't stop thinking of how fast he had been spinning completely out of control while clinging to the rope; it made him dizzy just remembering it, and he was hesitant to try it again. The pilot was waiting though, and he had to quickly get over his fear and climb on.

After buckling himself into the harness he gave the "go" sign to the pilot, and as they lifted off the rope slowly began spinning Rod again. He wasn't willing to spend another nauseating 10 minutes flying through the air and began hauling himself up the rope, knot by knot. He climbed until he reached the skid, unafraid now because of the attached safety harness, and with a final burst of effort heaved himself onto the skid and into the aircraft. The pilot swerved, surprised by Rod's sudden appearance, nearly throwing him back out the open door.

The second pickup had gone much more to Rod's liking; he hopped out as they touched down, feet on the solid ground and feeling a lot better about the trip and the possibility of repeating it during harvest.

Shortly after, Rod hiked in to spend several days picking and drying the buds. He had erected a small wooden frame covered in a tarp to keep his tools out of the rain, and now he ran lengths of fishing line across to hang the weed as he cut it. Final drying and trimming would take place at his house after he packed it all down the mountain.

While just dropping off supplies, it was easy enough for the seasoned helicopter pilot to work by himself; now with multiple canvas duffel bags of buds to be lifted into the hovering craft, each weighing around 50 pounds, a third person had to be added to the team. Rod recruited James, the veteran hang-glider and big-wave surfer, who was not afraid to lean out the helicopter door and reel in the harvest.

Rod stood on the ground hooking bags to the line, one at a time. James, tethered to the interior of the helicopter, pulled them up and stacked them in the rear passenger seats. When they had loaded all the marijuana that was ready, they flew down and unloaded the bags into Rod's truck, delivering them to his house. Rod, meanwhile, scurried down the mountain with his oversized backpack stuffed full and unpacked all the bags before the plants could mold. He set up a trimming station in his kitchen, and strung fishing line across the rooms of his house for final drying before he began weighing and making up individual plastic bags in different sizes for sale.

117

His house began to resemble his first boat, years ago now, which had been filled with so many burlap sacks of marijuana that he had to sleep on top of them.

The men spent weeks gathering all the pot from the mountain, and during this time, the only person allowed at Rod's house was James. Buds hung in every room, clippings littered the floors, and the strong smell was unmistakable. There was no way he could hide his activities from guests, and the parties had to stop for a couple months.

CHAPTER SEVENTEEN

With harvesting out of the way, Rod reset the garden again. He added compost, trimmed the plants he would be keeping, and planted more seedlings to replace the ones that weren't thriving. With his irrigation system working properly and his fence repaired, he could leave for a few weeks at a time while he waited on the next buds to form.

When he didn't have to be in the mountains, Rod resumed his normal pursuits: surfing and flying to Mexico to transport kilos of cocaine. This was his life for almost 10 years, and he loved every minute of it. He was bringing in close to $40,000 each month and continued to bury nearly half of that in his yard as the years went by.

I didn't have much spare time during these years and went about a decade without seeing him in person, although we kept in touch with our semi-regular phone conversations. Rod was always interested in how my children were doing; not having any of his own, he loved being an uncle to everyone else's.

I was on track to become head of the cardiology department at the hospital — the position I believe my parents whispered in my ear the day I was born. My normal work week was 60 - 70 hours, and I missed most of the milestones in my children's lives. Alicia had decided to be a permanent full-time mother to our two kids, which I was happy about — even if I didn't get to spend time with them, they would never have to spend their days with a babysitter or come home from school to an empty house and reheat leftovers.

Alicia had wanted more children, and we could definitely afford them, but I wanted to stop at two. I could barely find time to get to know the ones I had, and I didn't want to double the number of people in my house I might never really know. I already felt enough guilt about treating my kids the same way my parents treated me, even though mine had a full-time mother at home.

We argued for weeks about how many children we should have. I knew I would lose the argument in the end, as I always did, and made the ill-advised decision to take an afternoon off work and get a vasectomy — without telling my wife. She would think me the dutiful husband, trying to give her what she wanted, and I could lessen my guilt about my shortcomings as a father. But I didn't foresee Alicia's growing depression when each month passed without conceiving. My actions created more guilt of a much worse kind, but the lie had gone on too long to make it right.

When both kids started attending school full-time, Alicia was lonely and bored, and became more and more distant. Eventually, I felt like I was living in a beautiful house full of strangers who barely felt my presence, or lack thereof.

Rod stopped by my house unannounced one day while I was at work. Alicia was at home and let him in for coffee, bored as she was; if she hadn't been so lonely she might have closed the door in his face. This was the first time they had ever met in person, and she was immediately taken by his wonderful smile, then by his charm when he started talking to her. He had an uncanny ability to make people feel important, and that's exactly what she needed at that moment.

He had just visited his mother and sisters and was on his way to Los Angeles to meet a supplier, a fact he didn't mention to Alicia. He had found a new source of pure cocaine from Peru — better, he was told, than any he had yet purchased — and was going to strap a couple kilos under his shirt and fly it to Kauai for his lawyer and real estate connections.

His visit with Alicia worked wonders for my relationship with him. Instead of being some guy I had known since childhood who engaged in questionable activities, he instantly became her confidant. It probably only took five minutes before she was crying on his shoulder and unburdening her woes of our increasingly unhappy marriage. I had to find this out from Rod, though, on our next phone call. All she said when I returned home from work was, "Your friend Rod stopped by." I pressed for details, but was given lukewarm leftovers and a cold shoulder instead.

But now it was acceptable to maintain my friendship with him, as long as Alicia got to speak with him as well. Eventually, he became something like a therapist to her, but neither of them would give me any specifics about their discussions, or even how frequently they spoke. I was pleased that she had someone she trusted to talk to, even if she was telling my secrets to my first friend; Alicia couldn't bear to speak of her unhappiness to the other mothers in our children's play groups. We looked like a perfect family on the rare occasions we went out together, and she diligently maintained that facade in public. At home, we barely spoke.

When Rod stopped by and met Alicia, he left before I

could get home; he had arranged to meet his new contact at the airport in Los Angeles. These were still the days of walking up to the gate to welcome arriving guests right off the plane, flowers in hand for your loved ones, and a handoff was made in the airport restroom before Rod walked to a different terminal to catch his own flight. He received the plastic-wrapped bundles through the gap under the stall, awkwardly secured them to his torso with the roll of duct tape he had in his carry-on, and handed over a paper bag of cash. The men went their separate ways.

He made the short trip to his gate and leaned against a wall to wait for his flight to board. He stood there as nonchalantly as he could with several thousand dollars' worth of cocaine under his brown corduroy jacket, happy-go-lucky and whistling a tune, without a care in the world — until he looked up and noticed armed police officers running in his direction.

Paranoia kicks you in the guts instantly when you see cops while breaking the law, no matter how well you've prepared and how well-hidden your activities — or so Rod told me, because I don't have any first-hand knowledge of drug-running. The moment you envision your imminent capture, that's all you can think about. *They know*, your mind shouts, and that's all you can hear.

He tried his best to remain calm, but all he could think about was being forced to the ground and searched, handcuffs biting into his wrists, the humiliation of being led through the airport as a criminal, his mother's disappointment seeing him through the plexiglass barrier of a prison visiting room, the neon orange jumpsuit he'd have to wear for many years in his future. His hands began to shake as the men approached, running at full speed. He clasped them behind his back so the tremors wouldn't be as noticeable, taking care that his jacket still hung loosely without outlining the bulges. The men seemed to be running toward him in slow motion, allowing his mind more time to conjure up ever-more detailed, humiliating images of his downfall.

As quickly as the thoughts had entered his mind, they were replaced with confusion when the officers unexpectedly ran past him. With a great sigh of relief, he turned to watch where they headed in case he still needed to make a run for it. And then he noticed a large crowd gathering, along with cameras and boom microphones.

As preoccupied as he was with what was strapped under his clothing, Rod hadn't noticed the signs posted throughout the airport. A movie was being filmed, and he was seemingly the only person who had been unaware. Taking in more details of the scene, he recognized Willem Dafoe signing autographs behind barricades Rod had walked past without recognition. He was filming *To Live and Die in LA*, the cops were merely actors, and Rod slowly slid to the ground as his legs gave way; the scare had physically drained the energy from his body.

This marked the first real thoughts Rod had of getting out of the smuggling business, or at least sticking strictly with marijuana which carried a much lighter prison sentence. He had a fortune buried in his yard, more money than he had ever hoped to make in his life, and he didn't need to take such great risks. But the thrill of getting away with it yet again and the money he would make selling the pure coke when he got back home was too great to overcome his recent worries of being caught. He knew his luck would hold out, and so he banished any of the fears that arose as he stood in the airport expecting to be arrested.

CHAPTER EIGHTEEN_

The cocaine he had purchased from Peru was a big hit with his clients. The luxury real estate market on Kauai was taking off as more wealthy people found the island to be the perfect retreat from their city lives, with acres of land available on which to build dream vacation homes. Rod found the demand for his product increasing as well, so he made frequent trips to Los Angeles to satisfy his clientele's need to supply high-end lifestyle parties in hopes of selling the new high-dollar homes.

Having less time to tend his garden in the mountains, he made the decision to quit growing pot on such a large scale. It was a lucrative business, but the time required for the operation was too great to keep up. He could make the same money with much less effort by keeping his real estate clients stocked, and they frequently purchased a kilo at a time from him. He sold his share of the helicopter and bought a new sailboat, and with a small withdrawal — by shovel — from his stockpile of cash, he spent a few months sailing the South Pacific and surfing; Fanning Island became a favorite destination, one that he would sail to over and over for years to come when he needed to get away.

About six months after closing down his garden in the mountains, he got word from mutual friends that his former pilot had been killed. After losing his job with Rod, he had taken over a smuggling operation between Jamaica and Florida; he got caught up in a long-standing drug war between rival gangs in Jamaica, and died when a bomb exploded in his plane on an abandoned runway.

Looking to try something new, Rod took a boat delivery job for a wealthy client. He was well-suited for the task, and it was completely legal, providing him with sailing time while he earned money. He hired John to be the captain for the 55-foot catamaran *Ho'okele* that was to be sailed from Kauai, where it was purchased, to the harbor in Santa Barbara. Rod wanted a relaxing trip, which was why he hired a captain, and declared himself the cook; he prepared gallons of spaghetti sauce and froze other meals so they could eat in style, supplemented with as much fresh fish as they could catch along the way. At the last minute, Tom, the boat's new owner, decided he wanted to make the trip with them to learn more about sailing before he took possession in California for family excursions.

Tom stood at 6'8" and weighed approximately 350 pounds. At first glance, he wasn't in great shape, but he didn't disclose any medical issues before the trip. Rod was hesitant to bring him aboard, but as the new owner paying Rod, Tom insisted. The trip was no longer the relaxing journey Rod had envisioned; he hadn't counted on someone aboard who would be constantly asking questions, or spending weeks in a confined space with someone he wasn't sure he would get along with. But Tom had a timetable, so they started the 2,600-mile journey across the ocean.

They sailed uneventfully for the first half of the trip, until the winds began to pick up. A squall was blowing toward them and gusts of 30 knots required more vigilance at the helm, but it wasn't anything Rod was worried about. He and John had both sailed through much worse weather, and the boat was recently refurbished and newer than anything Rod had ever sailed. It was a good time to show Tom some of the finer points of sailing in less-than-ideal conditions. Suddenly, Rod and John realized they hadn't seen Tom in the past few hours.

Although the 55-foot boat was spacious, there weren't many places Tom could go unnoticed, so John went below to invite him to take his place at the helm for a lesson. He found Tom in his cabin, lying on his bed in a pool of blood. He ran back to Rod to report what he saw, downplaying Tom's condition, and said, "We should just let him be; I'm sure he'll be fine, and we're over halfway there already."

Rod went down to look in on Tom shortly after and found his entire bed soaked in blood. Tom was barely conscious and didn't respond to Rod's questioning. He had no visible wounds, and Rod couldn't determine where all the blood was coming from. He ran back up to the helm, ready to call for medical assistance.

"If we don't call for help he's going to die," Rod said. He tried a few channels on the radio with no success in communication.

"We have to activate the EPIRB," he said, and reached over to the Emergency Position Indicating Radio Beacon to switch it on.

John put a hand out to stop him. "Are you sure this is necessary?"

Rod activated the beacon without hesitation, frightened at what he had witnessed in Tom's cabin, and couldn't understand why John was so reluctant when a man's life was in jeopardy.

Before the trip had begun, John was assigned the task of getting an EPIRB for the boat, a mandatory piece of safety equipment for all boats in case of emergency. When activated, either manually or automatically when it touches water in the case of a sinking, it transmits a distress message and coordinates via satellite for Coast Guard or Navy search and rescue teams. When an EPIRB is purchased, it is registered with information about both the owner and the boat. John had thought to add several hundred dollars to his paycheck by stealing the EPIRB he brought onboard, never imagining they would need to activate it on such a routine crossing he had done many times before. The Coast Guard would know it was stolen if it had to be used.

The boat was 1,400 miles into the journey, the wind was steadily increasing, and one of the crew, the boat owner, was in serious trouble. With the beacon now activated, they could do nothing but stay on course and do their best to keep Tom comfortable and hope help arrived in time.

A Coast Guard C-130 aircraft was sighted three hours after they sent the distress call, and after a few tries Rod was able to get the rescuers on the radio. He explained they had a dying man onboard who couldn't get off his bed, not the sinking boat that they were looking for. The pilot acknowledged the situation and veered off to locate the nearest freighter with medics aboard to take Tom for emergency care, a standard maritime procedure. They located one not far off.

John was given coordinates and guided the boat to the freighter; he steered to the leeward side of the massive ship. The wind was still blowing hard and both vessels were rocking in the choppy waves. While pulling closer alongside, a rolling wave tilted the smaller boat and the spreader struck the side of the freighter, but it didn't break. John steered away and circled to make another pass a little lower, but had to reposition again due to the high seas. On the third pass, and finally on the radio with the freighter, they were able to secure the vessels together and coordinate to bring one of the freighter's medics aboard. Rod and John couldn't keep the boat steady and lift the 350-pound man off his bed without help.

The medic, also a sailor, assessed the situation and radioed the captain of the freighter for what was needed. The ship's crew rigged pallets in a heavy-duty net, since Tom was too big to fit in a standard litter, and lowered the contraption from a 70-foot crane. While John kept the boat steady at the helm, Rod and the medic wrestled Tom out of his bunk, dragged him up the few stairs, and laid him into the waiting net on deck. The pallets shifted as the boat lurched in the waves, and Tom, leaking more blood, rolled around from side to side as the men tried repeatedly to secure him. They managed to tie him to the pallets and signaled the crew on the freighter; the crane slowly reeled in the steel cable, hoisting the net, with Tom and the medic inside, from the deck.

The net swung wildly as it ascended; large waves from the storm rolled the freighter and Tom became a pendulum between the ship and the boat. The net snagged the spreader; Rod used an extended boat hook to catch the bottom of the net and, with the help of the medic hanging on inside, they dislodged it and began lifting again before the net could become permanently entangled or the mast could be broken.

The freed net swung even more violently and thumped into the side of the ship; the medic scrambled to the far side and barely held on. Tom was thrown upside down, still tied to the pallets, with his feet lodged in the top of the net. The crane reeled in the cable as fast as it could, and with one more swing, the net cleared the freighter's deck and Tom dropped onboard in a heap. Although not ideal, it was better than risking him hitting the crane's boom or other machinery on the deck if they tried to lower him gently.

With Tom safe on the freighter, the lines were released and Rod and John sailed away toward Santa Barbara. Tom's safety was out of their hands and they were worried but relieved; the medic on the freighter could do much more to help him until he could be airlifted to a hospital. Rod vowed he would never allow an owner to accompany him on a boat delivery again; from then on he would only sail long distances with people he knew personally, and unlike his *Old Salt* crewmate Craig, could keep a cool head in an emergency.

Rod and John sailed another 12 days to reach Santa Barbara and deliver the boat as promised. Rod got in touch with Tom's wife when they arrived at the harbor to arrange for the final payment. To their surprise, Tom accompanied his wife to the dock to meet them — he had spent 10 days in the hospital, and looked completely recovered. He took them out to dinner.

Rod found it hard to believe that a man who had been so near death such a short time ago could be out on the town so quickly, and plied him with questions. While he wouldn't disclose the medical condition that had left him in such bad shape, the men did find out that Tom was a high-ranking government employee. When the crew of the freighter radioed for a medivac after being unable to help him, Tom asked that they pass along his identification as well. Two military helicopters were dispatched immediately to pick him up and take him directly to a hospital in California, probably at a cost of millions to taxpayers.

Upon hearing this new information, Rod and John ordered

the most expensive items on the menu — on Tom. When settling the bill for the boat delivery, Rod decided to charge him for the homemade spaghetti sauce as well; Tom's wife made him pay for it, thinking it was the least he could do for his rescue at sea.

CHAPTER NINETEEN

After owning his house in Kapaa for nearly 20 years, Rod found a large piece of property in Lawai and, with a partner, bought 30 acres. They divided the acreage; Rod took seven and began building a home. Rod had been steadily burying money in his yard over the years; although he did have a bank account, he rarely used it, so he began digging up piles of plastic-wrapped cash to finance the building before he sold the Kapaa house.

Over the years, he had made millions of dollars but lived frugally in terms of material possessions. He didn't own exotic cars or multiple boats, and was quite good at selling what he owned for what he originally paid for it when it came time to upgrade. The vast majority of the money he spent was on parties and travel. Rod's favorite pastime was entertaining friends, old and new, and he spared no expense in providing the best food and drinks at his many gatherings. The same applied to his frequent travels, both for surf trips and smuggling runs. With his generous and outgoing nature, he instantly made new friends wherever he was in the world and showed them a good time. He bought and sold and gave away custom surfboards on a regular basis when he couldn't bring them home with him from overseas, having only used them for a few weeks.

"Why do you have so many washing machines?" a friend asked while helping Rod clean out his house in Kapaa.

He had purchased so many appliances on his smuggling runs to Mexico and South America, stuffing them with cocaine and shipping them to Kauai, that he no longer had any friends who didn't already have new ones. They gathered dust behind his house under a tarp, still in their original boxes. The men loaded them into Rod's truck and made several runs to the Salvation Army to give them away; he had no need for so many at his new house.

Rod stared at his friend in pretend bewilderment at the question. "Doesn't everyone?"

Rod's intention was to move everything from Kapaa to a large metal storage building he had erected on the new property and travel until the main house was constructed and ready to move into. He bought a new boat, a custom-built 36-foot Cape George cutter rig with teak decks christened *Windchaser*, to sail and surf in the South Pacific for a few months.

When he was nearly finished moving his possessions, he began digging up his pirate's treasure to secure in the storage shed and on his boat. He never thought to draw himself a map of the many locations in his large yard where he had buried the cash. Most of the holes had grown over after having lain in place for so many years. Being at least slightly drunk each time he went out to dig in his yard at night to hide more money, he really couldn't remember where it all might be. He spent dozens of evenings with a shovel and vodka-cranberry cocktails searching. Finally satisfied that he had retrieved the bulk of it, Rod put the house up for sale; multiple offers came in immediately as word of his late-night activity had spread through the years. Knowing that often-inebriated Rod could be a bit forgetful, prospective buyers jumped at the chance to search for hidden treasure.

The man who bought Rod's house spent a good deal of time digging through the yard. He did uncover small, forgotten stashes, but not as much as he'd hoped. When his grandchildren were young he employed them to dig holes, and much of the backyard was then converted to gardens. He occasionally still digs the odd hole, as several thousands of dollars was never accounted for in Rod's hazy memory.

Rod had been dating a woman for two years when he decided to move. Like his ex-wife, she had loved the lifestyle he provided, but eventually went beyond what Rod considered acceptable drug use. She had wrecked three cars and was always upset when he took off to go surfing by himself. He saw the end of their relationship coming, but had been unable to break it off; she wouldn't leave his house and Rod felt bad about throwing her out when she depended upon him for everything.

When the sale closed and the storage shed was packed, Rod and his girlfriend were at the dock preparing to leave for their extended sail. He hadn't seen any way out of bringing her, and was depressed about the idea of spending so much time on a small boat with a woman he no longer got along with, and who was quite destructive when she was angry. When he had purchased the new boat, she had gotten high and tried to sink it, thankfully failing because she had only thought to use a hammer. The damage was minimal and easy to repair, though time-consuming.

The couple scurried around *Windchaser* making the myriad last-minute preparations to sail first to Mexico. When all was finally ready, Rod asked her to run to the store for an extra carton of cigarettes in case they ran into bad weather and were delayed. He watched her walk down the dock to his truck and drive out of the parking lot. When the truck was out of sight, he ducked below and grabbed her bags, hauling them out onto the dock. He raised the mainsail, cast off the lines, and sailed away before she returned from her errand.

She can keep the truck, he thought. *She'll probably just wreck it anyway.*

Rod felt bad about leaving his girlfriend that way, but the alternative of spending many months alone with her was too terrible to consider. He cried for the first few days of the trip, both for the mess his relationship had become and shame about the way he dealt with it. He made the decision to quit dealing in hard drugs, seeing for the second time how they had destroyed a woman he loved.

CHAPTER TWENTY

R od had no regrets about discontinuing his importation of cocaine. He himself hadn't used it in years, sticking with alcohol and cigarettes as his vices, but the addictions and behavior of his former girl-friend opened his eyes to what was going on around him.

When he returned to his new house in Lawai after many months surfing abroad, he noted how many of his friends were now divorced and no longer had contact with their fami-lies. Their beautiful houses were gone and high-paying jobs lost, all due to what had started as an occasional party drug. When it all began, no one had suspected it would become their downfall and a new, sad way of life.

People turned to Rod for handouts, a few showing up at his new house looking haggard and unhealthy. He cooked for them and sent them home with extra food, and helped them get their lives back in order.

He willingly gave up the wealth cocaine had generated for him, but he couldn't reconcile his conscience with the damage his business had done. We spent many hours on the phone talking through his actions and their consequences.

"Were you the only person they bought cocaine from?" I asked.

"No … "

"Were you the only person who brought cocaine to the island?"

"No …"

"Did you introduce them to the heroin or meth they started using as well?"

"No …"

"Did you ever force anyone to start using drugs?"

"No …"

"You have some responsibility for providing easy access to cocaine, but people are going to do what they're going to do, whether you're involved or not," I told him. "If you want to ease your conscience, get your friends help. Pay for rehab for the ones who are willing to go."

And he did. Money was never a goal in his life, and since he had so much, he paid it little attention. Now he dug it out from its hiding places and put it to good use, trying to ease his burden of guilt. It helped a little, but not entirely. Nothing he did for the rest of his life could completely erase the destruction he helped bring to his friends' lives.

CHAPTER TWENTY-ONE

R od spent the next few years surfing; he sailed back and forth between Mexico, Fiji, and Fanning Island, only returning to Kauai when he had a shipment of marijuana to deliver. Despite lingering guilt about his involvement with cocaine, Rod had never had any qualms about pot. He hadn't used it himself in many years — sticking to his favorite legal vices — but he could never understand why it was illegal, and no one he knew had lost homes or families from weed alone.

Since he was sailing, and not going through airports or shipping appliances, Rod had to come up with a new way to conceal his cargo. He was aware of increasingly heavy Coast Guard patrols, and now in his 50s, the risk of incarceration was weighing on his mind like never before. He had never been caught — indeed he'd never even been suspected or searched — but after smuggling for more than 30 years, rumors of his activities spread as his contacts grew. While he never flaunted his occupation or his wealth, he could feel his time coming to end and acted more carefully than ever.

Throughout the South Pacific and Mexico, Rod purchased

windsurfing boards as large as he could find in the range of seven to nine feet in length. He cut them open and hollowed them out, replacing the foam cores with vacuum-sealed bags of marijuana. From his years repairing his own surfboards, he could easily reseal the boards, now filled with contraband, well enough to pass a fairly close examination if necessary. He spent many anxious late nights on foreign docks working on his boards with the tools he carried in his boat.

Strapped to the deck of his boat, he could carry boards containing 250 pounds of marijuana, and with the proper paperwork for importing sporting equipment, he would have no trouble with a routine inspection. Timing his arrivals back on Kauai to late nights, he was never stopped.

The boards were fairly destroyed after being cut open twice, first to remove the core and stuff them, then a second time to remove the contents, but he gave them away to anyone who wanted them. The majority of the boards got stacked in a pile in his storage shed, and Rod thought one day when he had more time to spend at his house, he'd build a decorative fence with them.

Rod called me one day in 2009, and for the first time his voice didn't have the purely optimistic tone that I was used to hearing throughout our years of friendship. He was beginning to doubt his ability to carry on without detection and was gearing up to make a final run to end his smuggling career. He was nervous, but he was determined to have a last hurrah.

"Rod, you're a professional. You've made the run to Mexico so many times you could do it in your sleep," I tried to reassure him. "Keep the faith for one last run and retire in style. You can do it."

He didn't sound very reassured and changed the subject. "How's Alicia? It's been a while since I got her on the phone."

I hesitated before answering, hoping the silence would provide the necessary information for Rod to come to his own conclusion and save me from saying it out loud. His silence outlasted mine, though.

"She left me."

With the kids grown and out of college, and starting their own families and careers, we no longer had anything in common. I had put my own career first, following the example from my parents, but having given up hers to raise our kids she had no choice but to create a separate life of her own over the years. I gave her everything she asked for in the settlement, and she moved to Northern California to be near Lucy, who was pregnant with her first child. I consoled myself by taking on more projects at work.

The morning after our call, Rod left for Mexico, anxious to get his final run under way. His destination was Puerto Vallarta, where he had made many contacts over the years, and he met some men from a cartel with 200 pounds of marijuana to sell. He hadn't dealt with these particular men before and when his shipment arrived, he found it to be damp, seedy weed — not his usual quality, and not worth the risk of bringing to Kauai for such small profit. The trip was off to a bad start.

Rod made the rounds of the town until he found another contact from a previous buy, and gave him the inferior weed.

"Find me the people who grow the very best weed, and this will be your payment," he told him. The man was happy to oblige.

The next day, he led Rod to a camp in the jungle outside Puerto Vallarta. Rod instantly regretted wearing shorts and a t-shirt; huge mosquitos swarmed him, biting and raising itchy welts on his exposed arms and legs. He worried about scorpions stinging his feet as he walked the dirt trail in flip-flops, having flashbacks from his first trip to Mexico as a teenager. He looked for snakes and jaguars, expecting doom around every clump of trees.

He swatted and itched his way along the jungle path behind his guide until they came to a large clearing dotted with crude wood and thatch shacks. As he was led into one of the buildings, he saw a table of stooped old ladies in bright peasant clothing trimming buds from huge piles of stems; the rafters were obscured by a previous harvest hanging to dry and awaiting manicuring. In all his years of coming to Mexico, he hadn't been invited into a processing area before, and was pleased with the level of trust it implied.

Rod went on a tour, drinking tequila and speaking with various workers he met along the way. They didn't know he was quitting the smuggling business and showed him the behind-the-scenes production, while getting him drunk to soften him up for a deal ensuring he would only buy bulk marijuana from them in the future.

Walking between two buildings, the men heard the far-off drone of helicopters. Without even a moment to confer with his guide, Rod sprinted for the closest patch of jungle. He had begun the trip with a feeling of dread, and the last place he wanted to be in jail was Mexico.

Peeking between the canopy trees, he saw military helicopters flying toward the camp and ran with no sense of where he was headed. He hadn't gone back the way he entered and never found the path toward town and the harbor; he could only rely on the position of the sun to guess the direction he was going. The jungle was thick, providing good protection for the buildings, and Rod got tangled in wild vines and his clothing was torn by brambles. Bloody scratches covered his body, staining his t-shirt as it ripped, but he feared slowing his pace to get away. Each new cut in his skin sobered him up a little more.

He blundered his way through the jungle for four hours; the mixture of sweat and blood on his skin only attracted more mosquitos. He watched for snakes and scorpions as best he could and managed to find a road, finally stopping to remove the thorns poking through the bottoms of his rubber flip-flops into the soles of his feet before continuing toward the docks a mile away.

Back on his boat, thirsty and exhausted, Rod hid below and pretended no one was home. He had nothing illegal on board, but he convinced himself that this was the trip on which he would finally be caught. He stayed on his boat for two nights while he made up his mind about what to do: find out what had happened to his guide and the workers at the camp and help them if he could, or simply go home empty-handed and retire. He decided to walk the path and bring his binoculars so if he got caught he could pretend he was a tourist on a birdwatching expedition through the jungle.

He was saved from another excruciating trip through the jungle when his guide appeared on the dock next to his boat, calling for him.

"Why did you run off?" he asked.

Rod was dumbfounded. "The helicopters. How did you get away?"

The man laughed. "Those are *our* police. They make a show of looking for drugs but instead provide protection. You ran so fast I couldn't catch you." He laughed again and flicked his cigar butt into the water next to the boat.

"We have 200 pounds nearly ready for you. Why don't you come with me and live in style until it is packed and ready? It will only be a couple more days."

Relieved to know he was not going to get busted doing

business with this cartel, Rod readily agreed to accompany his guide. He got in a large black SUV with tinted windows and enjoyed his first bit of air conditioning in many weeks as they drove through town. At the outskirts, they pulled up to a guard shack in front of an ornate steel gate; verifying the identity of the driver, the uniformed guard unlatched the gate and swung it open to let them pass into the grounds. The thick adobe walls enclosed several houses connected by walking paths, manicured lawns, and fountains — true Mexican wealth.

Rod and his guide were joined by a third man, a very large man who did not speak but followed in their footsteps as Rod was shown around the villa. Large paintings and intricately woven tapestries covered the walls of the many rooms, vases perched on pedestals, and the men made their way to a bedroom in which Rod's duffle bag was placed next to the bed.

"This will be your room, Jack Sparrow," his guide said. "I will be back in an hour; why don't you take that time to refresh yourself?"

The guide left, closing the door behind him. Rod poured himself a drink from the selection of bottles in the room and took a shower. With more than half an hour left until his guide returned, he thought he'd wander around the grounds and perhaps sit under one of the large trees and read the book he had brought. He opened the door to leave and encountered the third man standing right outside, blocking his way.

Rod realized at that moment that he was essentially a prisoner in the beautiful villa, not a guest.

This trip can't get any worse, he thought, and sat back on the bed with a fresh drink to await his guide.

He was at the villa for two days, and enjoyed beautifully prepared meals and tours of the grounds, but was never allowed to leave his room unaccompanied. He watched *Pirates of the Caribbean* in Spanish with several of the men in a viewing room with a big screen and plush recliners. They loved that he was sailing solo, and that his cheerfulness reminded them of the main character. They had all called him Jack Sparrow since his arrival, and Rod was certain they neither knew nor cared what his real name was.

In their deal with the local authorities, the cartel was not permitted to load marijuana onto customers' boats within sight of the harbor, preserving the image that the cops kept the town free of illegal activities. Rod was asked about his next destination.

"I'm headed to San Blas next," he told his guide. "Thought I'd do some surfing before I sail home."

"We will find you there," he was told, and driven back to the harbor. "In four days, sail three miles directly west of town and we will load your boat."

Rod was confused, wondering why he couldn't have been surfing the entire time he waited, but was glad for the interesting new experience — being a "guest" in a villa owned by a Mexican drug cartel was not an everyday occurrence, but one he hoped he'd never have again. He set sail and made the 100-mile journey north, happy to get back in the ocean.

Rod set anchor outside a beautiful right-hand wave and spent a pleasant three days surfing and drinking cocktails on his boat. On a supply run into town, he bumped into an acquaintance from years ago who was closing the bar he owned before moving back to the States.

"I have a couple crates of booze to get rid of. Do you want them?" he asked.

Taking this as a sign that the bad luck of the trip was over, Rod readily agreed to take them off his hands. He borrowed some rope and tied the crates to the nose of his surf board, making two extra trips around the surf and stashing the bottles on his boat. Top-shelf margaritas for the way home!

He awoke early on the fourth day to get in a final surf session before he began the sail back to Kauai. Still in the water, he noticed a twin-engine rubber pontoon approaching his boat at high speed; it bumped up against his cutter rig and a man climbed aboard, catching a line from the smaller boat and securing them together.

Rod paddled furiously out past the break to get back; a second man began handing black duffle bags from the pontoon up onto the deck of Rod's boat before he could get there, and the first man carried them to the bow and arranged them in a pile.

"I thought we were meeting three miles out!" Rod yelled as he closed the final distance and climbed the ladder, throwing his surfboard onto the deck. "People on the beach can see us."

"We are in an unexpected hurry," was the reply. "We have taken care of any problems that might arise from being seen."

And with that, the men finished loading; Rod passed them the bag full of cash, and he cast off the line holding the boats together. The men sped off.

Rod went forward to inspect his new cargo. When he hefted the first duffel, it felt much heavier than it should have; digging through the sealed bags full of beautiful spears of marijuana, he uncovered iron bars at the bottom. The men had loaded these in case Rod needed to dump the load along the way — the bags would quickly sink, possibly sparing him capture and making it unnecessary to give up his source.

Already resupplied for his long sail back to Kauai, Rod pulled up the anchor and pointed his boat toward home.

CHAPTER TWENTY-TWO

T he 42-day journey back to Kauai started off quite pleasantly, with good weather and a steady wind. Rod sat at the helm and sipped a drink, reading a book. He was in a hurry to complete this final smuggling trip and had fired up the engine for more speed. Thinking the worst was behind him, he lounged on the deck enjoying the beautiful sailing weather without a care in the world.

With only a few days left to get home, the engine began to sputter, pulling Rod out of his pleasant, tipsy daydreaming. After a quick inspection he determined his filters were clogged and needed changing. He could have sailed the remaining few days without his engine, but he wanted to be prepared in case of an emergency and he had the spare parts on board.

Rod slipped a disposable white mask over his mouth so he wouldn't breathe fumes as he worked. Crouched next to the engine with his tools, sweating in the hot sun wearing only a ragged pair of board shorts, he was so intent on getting the job done quickly that he didn't notice the boat that crept up next to him after slowly circling. A short horn blast got his attention, and he looked up to see a Navy boat; as a supplement to the Coast Guard due to increased drug traffic, the Navy had begun a regular patrol of the route between Mexico and Hawaii looking for boats carrying contraband.

Rod stood frozen, once again imagining his doom. He hadn't carried the big black duffel bags below, and they sat on deck, glaringly conspicuous to him. Still wearing his mask, he waved to the men, not knowing what else to do while he waited to be boarded and hauled off to prison. Rod had a case of Coke nearby and held out some cans as an offering, hoping a friendly gesture might help.

The men standing on the patrol boat didn't see a smuggler with hundreds of pounds of marijuana piled on the deck of his boat; they saw a tired, unkempt man, sweating profusely and wearing a medical mask. The swine flu had recently claimed the world's attention as a new epidemic and the men were reluctant to board his boat in case he was sick. Rod had the appearance of someone very ill after working under the hot sun for so long. From a distance, the bags of marijuana looked like ordinary sail bags, normal for any sailor to store on deck. Pulling up close, they shouted to him to see if he was okay or if he needed medical attention, and refused the cans of soda Rod still held out. Rod coughed dramatically a few times when it dawned on him why he wasn't about to be boarded, and answered that he was fine to continue on his own. The patrol boat veered off and motored away.

A couple hours passed before Rod's hands stopped shaking enough to finish the engine repairs. Once again, he marveled at his luck and was happy he would be retired in a few short days and never again feel the dread of imminent incarceration. He went back to work on the engine, knowing that after his recent brushes with the law he was home free.

For his final trip, he had decided to sail into Hanalei Bay

on Kauai's north shore to unload; the swells were down for the summer and getting into the bay would be easier than sailing to the south shore. Only a few days out, he changed his heading to direct north so it would appear he was inbound from California, not Mexico, just in case anyone else was watching for him. The change added extra time to the crossing, but he was playing it safe. He attached one of the duffels of pot to a line and tossed it overboard to test how fast it would sink if he needed to dump the load; the bag was too full of air and simply floated on the surface, even with the metal bars inside. He reeled it back in, knowing that if he were stopped and inspected he wouldn't be able to pretend the bags weren't his. He poured another drink and tried to banish worry from his mind.

After sailing past the other Hawaiian Islands, Rod waited well offshore until after nightfall so he wouldn't be seen arriving back on Kauai. He set his anchor in the bay and paddled to the beach on his surfboard, then hitched a ride to town to get in touch with James, who would be driving a zodiac out to the boat to unload. He bought a case of beer at the grocery store, hitchhiked back to the beach and paddled back to the boat. Pulling up his anchor, Rod sailed approximately 10 miles out of the bay and waited. Word had been spreading of his activities and his long absence from the island would now be noticed, whereas in the past he could easily pass off his trip as just another surf expedition. People had long since begun to wonder how he could have such a beautiful house and throw such lavish parties when it didn't appear he had a job; not everyone who came to his house was a friend.

James met him a few hours later, shortly before sunrise, and together they offloaded the heavy duffels onto the zodiac. Rod hadn't thought to remove the iron from the bags and the tiny boat was way over its rated weight capacity; since it was so close to sunrise, there wasn't time for two trips and they crossed their fingers James would reach shore with his load intact.

James departed. He had parked his truck on the far end of the beach and could easily drive the borrowed zodiac onto the trailer by himself and haul the entire load back to Rod's house. He motored the 10 miles slowly and arrived in the bay just as the first colors were painting the sky. The beach was still deserted as he transferred the bags to the truck bed, cursing Rod with every bag he moved because of the extra weight.

Rod decided to sail back into the bay and relax for a few days before heading to his berth at Nawiliwili. He was officially retired, and would throw a party on his boat in Hanalei to celebrate. Relief at finally being home, and home free, flooded through his body as he guided the now-empty sailboat into the bay once again.

Hanalei Bay is normally crowded with boats in summertime; taking advantage of the flat water, beautiful scenery, and summer vacation, people spend weeks living on their boats in the shallow water, some locals and some sailors from far-off destinations. Being a well-known man, Rod's arrival after sunrise was noticed by many who wished him a happy return from his trip, but he was also noticed by a jealous few who wanted to see his downfall. Unaware that someone had radioed the police to report a boat loaded with drugs, Rod dropped his anchor and sat on deck enjoying the remainder of his case of beer for breakfast before he went to town to get supplies for his party.

As Rod greeted friends who swam up to his boat and invited them to come over that evening for a party, two Coast Guard vessels sped through the bay and stopped on either side of him, sirens wailing. The men threw lines to Rod and announced he would be boarded under suspicion of smuggling contraband, then they came aboard ready to make an arrest. They had been told he was the biggest smuggler in the islands.

They tore Rod's boat apart for hours, checking and rechecking every compartment and hatch, slicing open his mattress and pulling out the stuffing, and ripping his spare sails out of their bags. They x-rayed the hull. His few clothes were scattered on the floor of his cabin and the icebox, now nearly empty after his long trip, held only a single onion. Rod finished his beer while he waited, confident for the first time that he had nothing to hide.

Angry at either being misinformed or missing the shipment of contraband, the Coast Guard still gave Rod a ticket. Stating that it was illegal to bring fruits or vegetables from Mexico, he was fined $15 for his onion. Rod never paid it.

CHAPTER TWENTY-THREE

W hen Rod returned to his house after his four-month absence, he learned his partner, who owned the majority of the property in Lawai, had died with his wife in a boating accident. His partner had willed his land to his adult children, and not having signed any official paperwork for the ownership of his share, Rod was suddenly dispossessed — he couldn't prove he owned any of the land.

After some half-hearted negotiation — Rod had lost interest in the property after his friend died — the children agreed to buy him out at only a fraction of what he had originally paid; they were not mean-spirited or trying to rob him, but they didn't know Rod or have any record of the original sale.

He packed up the few items he wanted from the house, dug up a few stashes of cash from the yard, and moved back onto his boat in the harbor. He didn't look for a new house; he was no longer growing pot and didn't need the land, and he decided it was a good time to explore more of the world on his boat and find new waves to surf.

True to his word, Rod officially retired from the smuggling business. The creeping thoughts of spending the rest of his life in prison disappeared, and he almost instantaneously reverted back to the happy, carefree person he had been since we were kids.

He sold *Windchaser* and purchased the *Noel Mae*, a custom 43-foot Polaris double-ender, one of only 13 ever made. He spent more time surfing and took twice-yearly trips to Fanning Island, sometimes spending two or three months there at a time. Instead of packing his boat with marijuana or cocaine, he went to Walmart and bought thousands of dollars' worth of school supplies and clothing to donate to the children of Fanning. He was still trying to ease his conscience from his years flooding Kauai with cocaine, and he had the money to make a difference in the lives of many less fortunate.

His arrival on Fanning had always been cause for celebration — in the past, he was a guy who threw great parties; now when he was spotted at the harbor children came running, knowing that he had a boat full of presents for them. Rod spent time at the schools and in the local families' homes getting to know everyone, not just other surfers and sailors.

Rod had always enjoyed his life, and that didn't change. Now he didn't have any of the anxiety caused by his former career, and concentrated his extra energy on family and friends.

CHAPTER TWENTY-FOUR

I finally retired too, giving up my position as head of the cardiology department at the hospital I had worked at since college. I had put off retirement until long after the usual age because I simply didn't know what else to do with my time; my childhood had been spent preparing for a career, and now that career was gone. I hadn't taken the time to learn any new hobbies or skills, and I wandered around my big, lonely house wondering what to do with so much unoccupied time. I visited my children and grandchildren, but they had lives of their own, and try as I might I couldn't force myself into their lives. Too much time had passed, and the resentment caused by my neglect could not be erased by any gifts I might bring. I had a great bedside manner and I was loved as a doctor by the people I treated, but that was only a superficial sort of love. I had never learned how to truly be a part of someone's life.

One day I called Alicia; the idea of rekindling our relationship had been on my mind for a while, and I wouldn't know if it was possible unless I tried. We had remained cordial through the years after our divorce, but couldn't be called friends anymore. She was the one person I had imagined growing old with, and I regretted losing her. I had gone on a few dates since we broke up, set up by colleagues who worried about me being alone, but I never thought I had the time to devote to a new relationship. Or, more accurately I should say, I never took the time.

Now I had nothing but time and no one to spend it with. I downed a small glass of single malt to calm my shaking hands and dialed Alicia's number. The first ring set my heart racing, transporting me back to my college years of working up the nerve to ask her out. My mind flooded with dreams of family — what I once had, and had willingly given away, could be rediscovered. It would be better than the best times we had shared, now that I knew what I wanted and had the time to make it happen. That first ring lasted long enough to encompass all the thoughts of my future, flashing through my mind and making the possibility of a new life seem almost certain.

She picked up on the third ring, surprised to hear from me. She sounded happy, and I automatically assumed it was due to hearing my voice. I took a deep breath and stated my case, without any fear of rejection. I knew we could make it work.

"Have you lost your mind?" she asked, laughing at me. "I put everything I had into our marriage, our children, and you treated it like it was nothing. You threw us away for your career, and never thought twice about it. I don't have anything left for you."

I muttered something like "Sorry for bothering you," and hung up, ashamed.

I had been so sure I could regain my former life, and my hopes were dashed in a matter of moments. I poured myself another drink and dialed Rod.

CHAPTER TWENTY-FIVE

I had only been to Kauai once before, on my honeymoon, now decades ago. Rod had given me directions to the harbor where he now lived again, and I found it easily enough, only minutes from the airport in my rental car. His boat sat at the end of a pier, bobbing slightly in the rippling water of the bay. A refreshing breeze blew away the heat of the blazing Hawaiian sun.

I had never spoken much about my innermost feelings to anyone, but on the day of Alicia's final rejection I had unburdened myself to Rod, sharing my guilt and shame, much as he had done with me some years ago. He invited me to take an extended vacation, something I had neglected for my entire life.

I paused halfway down the pier, sad and a little depressed. I should have done this when my children were young. I should have taken trips with my family and learned about the world alongside them. I should have taken the time off of work. I should have known what was really important.

I should have…

I should have…

But it was too late now, and the full impact of being alone hit me while I stood there, staring at Rod's boat. Here I was, approaching 70 years old with nothing but money to show for the life I had lived. I wondered if Rod felt the same way, also divorced and without a family. I closed my eyes and took a deep breath, taking in the salty scent of the place, and continued walking.

When I arrived, Rod was busily preparing lunch for us — fish tacos and homemade guacamole. He poured me a vodka-cranberry cocktail after greeting me with a hug, and showed me around his boat — his home — small and crammed with mementos from his years of travels. The galley, where he had spent countless hours preparing meals for himself and his friends, wasn't even the size of my walk-in shower, and didn't have an electric refrigerator — he had to drive to the grocery store every other day for a bag of ice to keep his food cold.

I knew Rod had made millions of dollars over his lifetime, and asked him where it all went.

"It's gone," he told me. "I spent nearly every penny I ever made, with just enough left over to pay my slip rent every month. I got sick last year and was in the hospital for over a month; I've never had health insurance, so that pretty much wiped out my savings."

We discussed his current health for a bit, and I assessed him with my doctor's eye. He looked pretty well for a man who had led the life he did.

"So here we are," I said, sitting in the cockpit of the boat in the sunshine. "This could be us 50 years ago, eating lunch together at school. So much has changed since then — but not really."

We were nearly exactly as we had been during our school days. I had plenty of money but was lonely, sitting with my one real friend. Rod had very little, but was surrounded by people who loved him. In the hour I had been on his boat, four people stopped by to see if he was home and say hello. Rod offered hospitality to everyone — a drink, tacos, or, "Come sit and meet my oldest friend." He had so little, but what he had he was ready to give away to anyone willing to stay and chat, asking nothing in return except friendship and maybe a story to entertain him.

"Do you regret losing all your money?" I asked. "If I had known earlier, I could have set you up with my investment guy; you could be living off the interest, with a nice, comfortable house."

"I didn't *lose* my money," he replied. "I spent it on family and friends, on adventures. I've seen the world so many times over, surfed thousands of beautiful breaks, and I've met people from different cultures and was invited into their homes. Hundreds of kids call me "Uncle" when I see them. What better things can money buy?"

He thought for a moment. "I have no regrets. I've always done exactly what I wanted to do. Collecting money was never my goal in life, and I was blessed to have enough when I needed it."

Rod descended the three steps into the galley to refresh our drinks, came back up and lit a cigarette, blowing the smoke up toward the mast. I watched him, sitting there in his worn surf shorts and t-shirt and thought we had come full circle to our childhood. Here I was, still in my neatly pressed travel clothes, new and barely worn. A sparkling new watch was on my wrist, a gift I had bought myself for retirement. Rod still didn't own a watch. This could have been the same day our 12-year-old selves had met in the cafeteria, the day of my very first wristwatch, *Flintstones*, or *Jetsons*, I still can't remember.

I pointed this out to Rod, and he laughed, and we recalled our early days together. Sharing rabbit and lobster for lunch. Climbing through the hills of Cardiff by the Sea and playing with an owl named Alfie. "The good old days," we agreed, clinking our glasses.

But those were Rod's good old days, Rod's stories. I had only been an observer while he went out and lived, and the world passed me by.

We sat in silence for a few minutes, each reminiscing about our lives. Rod smiled, a twinkle in his eyes, and looked up at me.

"You have regrets, I can tell," he said as I blinked to keep a tear from escaping. "It's never too late to be what you want to be. What do you want to do when you grow up?" He laughed.

"I don't know."

A rich, lonely, 60-something was not what I envisioned in my childhood.

"Then welcome to the first day of the rest of your life," Rod said. "It's a beautiful day for an adventure. The trades are blowing and the ocean is smooth, and I've got a full bottle of vodka down below. Let's go sailing and throw out the lines, maybe catch a fish for dinner. Tomorrow I'll teach you how to surf. The only thing that matters right now is *right now*."

We cast off the lines, raised the main, and sailed together until sunset every night for two weeks.

CHAPTER TWENTY-SIX

Those two weeks sailing with Rod began a new chapter in my life. He assumed the role of teacher and therapist; after a day of hands-on instruction and a lexicon of boat jargon, I had the helm for the remainder of our time. Rod was free to do what every good bartender does throughout the world — he listened to my fears and troubles while loosening my tongue with cocktails. He sat quietly as I examined my conscience aloud, with the occasional "sheet in" or "tack here."

"It sounds to me like you need to go out in the world and do something good," he determined as my planned vacation time came to an end, although I really didn't have to be anywhere anymore. "Let's sail to Fanning and you can experience for yourself how uplifting it is to do charity work. It'll be good for your soul."

I gave Rod enough cash to stock the boat with both food and new clothing for the children of the island, along with a list of basic first-aid supplies like bandages and peroxide in case my medical skills might be needed, then flew back to the mainland to prepare my life for an extended leave. My housekeeper and her husband moved into my house as caretakers, and a visit to my lawyer ensured that my estate would go to my ex-wife and children if the ocean crossing didn't go as planned.

"You're not a young man anymore," my lawyer pointed out. "Is this really the time to start visiting third-world countries? By boat?"

I must be out of my mind, I thought, and without Rod nearby to keep me motivated I realized I was indeed too old for such a trip. I would go home and write a large check to a charity, and maybe that would be enough to soothe my soul. I left my lawyer's office feeling more depressed than ever.

Shortly after arriving home and locating my checkbook, I received a text from Rod.

The children are going to be so happy to see you! When will you be back? We're stocked and ready to sail!

I smiled at the message; it was as if it came from the universe to allay my fears. I looked around my big, empty house — if I stayed, I would be killing time, by myself, until I simply ran out of time. I would only be adding to the list of "should haves" that were already troubling my soul.

Now or never.

I took a deep breath, and with my exhale I picked up my bags, closed up the house, and opened the door to a world full of possibility.

ACKNOWLEDGMENTS_

Many thanks to Soren Velice for his editing talents. A former print journalist, Soren has edited all four of my books, and hopefully many more to come. He has helped me become a better writer through the liberal and judicious use of his red pen.

A huge thank you to Donna Burovac for her keen eye for detail.

Mark - I couldn't have written this without you! Thanks for not letting me quit. You and Randy and boat drinks will always be some of my favorite memories.

Thank you to Ben Silver for his patient explanations of helicopters, and Andy Buoni of 3 Dogs Farm for his immense knowledge of growing marijuana (and how much would fit in small spaces).

Thanks also to Mike and Andy for your stories.

Finally, thank you to my test readers for their comments and encouragement — Clare Burovac, Mary Burovac, Cynthia Dazzi and BJ Elessar.

Cover design by Don Schlotman

Cover photo by Melissa Burovac

Author photo by Shanti Manzano

ABOUT THE AUTHOR_

Melissa Burovac is a writer and ocean photographer living on the Big Island of Hawaii. An avid outdoorswoman, she enjoys paddling – one-man, six-man and SUP – surfing, scuba diving, swimming, yoga and running. She is always ready for adventure and loves doing things that scare her a little.

wanderwithmelissa.com

facebook.com/melissaburovacwriter

twitter.com/m3lissab33

Made in the USA
Columbia, SC
06 November 2018